SAN DOMINGO
The Medicine Hat Stallion

BY MARGUERITE HENRY

Illustrated by Robert Lougheed

SCHOLASTIC INC.
New York Toronto London Auckland Sydney

Acknowledgments:

The verse on page 34 is the *Centenary Edition of the Poems of Emily Dickinson*, published by Little Brown & Company, 1930.

The verse on page 96 is excerpted from "The Sailor's Hornpipe" in *Irish Songs and Airs* by Elizabeth L. Gallagher and Carlo Peroni, published by E.G. & Co., 1936.

ISBN 0-590-48638-1

12 11 10 9 8 7 6 5 4 3   4 5 6 7 8 9/9

Printed in the U.S.A.   40

First Scholastic printing, October 1994

*Dedicated with love to
Robert O'Breaslain
of County Donegal, Ireland*

Contents

Part I. The GANGLINGS

The Strange Letter   9

The Fierce God   18

The Shooting Match   25

The Halt and the Lame   34

The Buscadero Belt   41

"Vengeance Is Mine"   49

War Bonnet and Shield   55

"I Hear Eyes..."   63

"Him Damn Lucky"   73

"Injun Gentled"   79

Part II. The TRANSIT

The Whirling Sky	86
Sodding Day	91
Royal Son of Ireland	101
Map of the Wild Lands	108
"If a Hand Be Four Inches..."	116
Pure Spanish Barb	121
Stranger on Horseback	132
The Withered Hand	141

Part III. The CRUCIBLE

The Handbill	148
Orphans Preferred	156
The Long Good-bye	161
"Take Your Druthers"	169
Deer Creek to Devil's Gate	175
The Scalp-lifters	182
A House Divided	192
War Paint	201
Ambush	210
"Forward Is the Ticket"	219

Part I. The GANGLINGS

The Strange Letter

HIS NAME is Peter Lundy and he has just turned twelve, and he thought the letter he'd found was meant for him. It began, *Dear, dear Peter . . .*

There was no mistaking his mother's fine, round handwriting, and it was like her to plant surprises in secret, yet where he'd be sure to find them. Sometimes he came upon a picture she'd sketched, or a piece of rock candy, or a riddle. And one merry Christmas, she made an Indian headdress of magpie feathers and hung it on the hatrack without a word. He knew from the way the headband fitted that she intended it for him. He wore it for weeks, even to bed. But never before had there been a letter.

His mother was always inventing ways for him to enjoy himself. Every spring when he caught the quinsy sore throat, like now, she planned exciting things for him to do. Last year she taught him to slit-braid rawhide into quirts and headstalls.

And this year—this very night when he was still abed but

practically well—she handed him her treasure chest with its gold hasp, and a gold key in the shape of a question mark. "Likely you'll laugh at my tomboy keepsakes," she said. "Some go 'way back to when I was eleven, twelve."

As Peter turned the key and lifted the lid, a curious feeling came over him. The treasures he saw might well have been his own—that is, if *his* father had permitted the hoarding of stones flecked pink and green, and a miniature nest that must have belonged to a hummer bird, and hairs from a horse's tail, and a blue-racer snakeskin. He was pleased to find a tiny exercise book with childish printing on the cover:

Historick Dates to Remember
Columbus landed in the New World 1492
First horses landed at Santo Domingo 1493

Funny, Peter thought, that his mother would care when or where the first horses landed. Or was it her schoolmaster who cared?

Rummaging deeper into the chest, he came upon a piece of oiled paper folded over several times. Gingerly he laid the paper open and found a coil of hair so silken he couldn't help stroking it with his fingertips. The color matched the gold of a California sorrel he'd once seen—not flaxen, like the mane or tail, but pure glinty gold. Now he spied a tag. In his mother's handwriting he read, *Peter Lundy. His first haircut. November 13, 1847. Age two years, eight months.*

Peter laughed to himself, blushing for admiring his own baby hair! He looked around the room to see if anyone were watching. But Grandma Lundy was dozing in her rocker, the almanac forked over her head like a tepee to shut out the firelight. Baby Aileen slept too, while his mother foot-rocked the cradle and worked on his new shirt. He noticed that his mother's hair almost matched the lock he held, except that hers was coppered some by the firelight.

He tucked the curl back into the paper and placed it where he'd found it. He was about to close the chest when his eye fell upon a pocket in the lid, and edging out of it the letter.

His excitement mounted as he unfolded it and saw the pictures flying across the pages. It was like finding a book written just for him. He settled deeper into bed, squirming and pawing like a dog until the cornhusks made a snug nest around him. He pulled up the buffalo robe covering. Then, holding the pages aslant to catch the candlelight, he began again:

Dear, dear Peter . . .

He could hear his mother say the words with a bird-lilt to her voice. But as he read on, a nameless fear spread over him. This didn't sound like her at all. Why, she was forever humming or singing, until Pa said she made him jumpy. Could it be that her happiness was all make-believe? He read the disturbing sentence again, wondering how anyone who sang most all day could write:

There is nothing half so sad as living. I feel like one forsaken . . .

Was the letter planted on purpose? Did his mother figure that writing him about her feelings was easier than talking them out?

. . . Jethro, as you know, has never been the same since that terrifying experience.

Why did she say *Jethro* instead of *your father?* And what experience did he have?

Far out on the plain a coyote wailed his thin, quavering note. Usually the sound sent him off to sleep, like the wind of the prairie. But tonight the familiar howl chilled him.

Peter longed to cry out, "Ma! Oh, Ma! What *was* it that happened to Pa?" But his throat choked on the words. The woolen sock around his neck was suffocating him. Having the quinsy used to be cozy; he felt isolated and free of his father. Would the "terrifying experience" explain why Pa seldom spoke —or else burst into rages?

Half fearful of learning more, yet driven by curiosity, Peter read on.

> *Jethro continues to brood over the past that scarred him. His anger toward the world grows instead of lessens. My heart comes into my mouth whenever he enters the house, for I never know if the bitterness will be in him. He does crazy-wild things then. The last time he stamped like a buffalo on my bleeding-heart bush that had just begun bearing necklaces of pink hearts. It was my strongest link with home. Remember how we used to open up the flowers?*

Anger suddenly welled in Peter. So that was it! That's what had happened to the bush his mother prized. Why, all summer everyone's leftover bath water was saved for the bleeding hearts. Grandma loved them, too. When they blossomed, she and Ma acted like children, taking one of the flowers apart to show Peter how each was made up of two pink rabbits, two Cinderella slippers, a pair of drop earrings, and a green bottle. His father, coming in unexpectedly one day, caught them separating the petals. "A fine thing to teach a lad!" he said, his eyes cold as glass. "If there's anything I can't abide, it's a milksop of a boy."

Peter remembered how his mother had gone to her loom then, giving no answer at all.

He read on.

How I miss the dear United States, and especially Syracuse. They seem far away as the moon. Sometimes I feel I'm drowning in an ocean of buffalo grass. From here at Rawhide Creek to the Laramie Mountains, as far as the eye can reach, there is not a tree in sight. Only a lone wild plum tree and a few willows weeping along the creeks that always seem either dry or flooding their banks.

Daily I watch the westward trek of covered wagons, and the weary emigrants expecting paradise around the next bend, or Indians! The footsore horses, mules, and oxen are the worst sufferers. It was not their idea to go West. Yesterday Peter and I saw a kitten actually riding on the face of a plodding horse. The kitten's hind paws were steadied on the horse's noseband. The two creatures seemed to take comfort, one from the other—somewhat the way young Peter and I do. He is the light of my life, and I never cease to wonder at the miracle of his understanding.

Peter swallowed hard. Suddenly he understood the letter was not his. It was intended for his *Uncle* Peter!

When I think of Peter's future, I tremble for him. He admires the strength of his father but is bewildered by his coldness one moment and his hot temper the next, and his constant criticism. Yet the boy manages to eke out his own happiness. He loves this great wild-horse country where the eagles nest. The prairie is his element, his school. In a howling gale he'll stand utterly still and listen, the way you and

I would to a symphony. He is fascinated, too, by the people —the hunters and trappers, the bullwhackers and mountain men, but most of all by the Indians. They are around us at all times. Peter drums and sings with them. They call him Yellow Hair and tousle him in affection.

Peter turned another page in guilty eagerness.

When Indians come to the house for food, I have no fear of them, but if we were to meet in the wilderness, I'd be terrified. The one time I saw Chief Red Cloud in a savage mood was the day someone stole his horse from our hitching rack. He caught the thief and revenge came swift and deadly.

Just last week some Sioux big chiefs, including Red Cloud, Red Dog and Brave Bear, broke bread with us. (It was more than bread, I might add.) I felt sorry for them, padding around in the morning chill with nothing to cover them but a breechcloth; so it did my heart good to watch them clean their plates of good nourishing rice with raisins and drink it down with a whole boilerful of hot coffee.

"Pooty damn good!" they said by way of good-bye, taking one of my spoons along with them and sheepishly returning it next day.

Baby Aileen and Grandma may waken at any moment, so I'll answer your questions in haste.

Peter glanced up, as if the letter were being written this moment. Aileen and Grandma were still asleep.

Yes! Jethro's Trading Post and Smithy is busy as a hive. Being on the westbound trail, there's a constant stream of wagons to mend, harness to repair, and animals to shoe. Peter and his Dalmatian are stout helpers, although Jethro doesn't admit it. The dog, a starveling named Dice, was given Peter by a gambler. He is quite a hypnotist, staring the horses into submission when they are being shod.

Don't worry about us in our soddy-house; it is warm in winter and cool in summer. At the moment it is falling into disrepair and will need fresh sodding before another winter. Sometimes a brave sunflower grows right out of the roof!

Your little niece, Aileen, is eight months old now, plump as a berry, with the dark hair and eyes of Jethro, who adores her.

Grandma Lundy has just turned eighty-six. She lives in a childlike world of her own. When Jethro rants and storms, she crawls into her cocoon and sleeps, or pretends sleep. Sometimes I think Peter is the most adult member of our family.

Peter was struck with the sudden knowing that children of the plains grow up quicker. If Ma thought of him as "adult," he'd ask right out, "What *was* the terrifying experience Pa had?" Just as soon as he read the one page that was left, he'd ask.

Please understand, dear brother, that I sympathize with Jethro's black moods—if only they didn't recur so often when I am tutoring Peter in reading, and we are both

*laughing over some droll saying of Rip Van Winkle's or
Natty Bumppo's. Someday, when Peter is old enough, I
shall tell him the whole hideous story. But oh! meanwhile,
why does Jethro have to look upon Peter as a competitor
for my affection? Certain it is I give my love to both, each
to his needs. I long to be a strong bridge between them,
but somehow the rift keeps widening until I am at a loss
which way to turn.*

*I've not spoken of this to anyone, much less written it.
An outrider stopped yesterday to say that Blodgett's Express would come flying by tomorrow, going east. So you
should receive this letter within the month. By then my life
may hopefully be better.*

*Your loving sister,
Emily*

*P.S. I still have our funny old glass cat. She sits by the
fire scaring away the mice in the night. And I love our old
clock that chimes the hours and the quarters.*

Peter blinked. He felt as if he had been reading forever,
and now was caught in a web so tight and sticky that nothing
could wrench him free. He folded and quickly hid the letter in
the pocket of the chest where he'd found it. He wondered why
it had never been sent. Did Blodgett's never come by? Did Ma
just stow away the letter and forget it?

He closed and locked the lid. He pinched the candle into darkness. Making no sound, he placed the chest on the stool beside his bed. Without saying good night, he turned face down into his pillow. Tears burned his eyes. He tried to swallow, but couldn't for the pain. It was not the quinsy anymore, but a deeper misery he couldn't understand. The mother he worshiped was keeping a secret locked away from him, a secret that might make him less afraid of his father. Or—the thought terrified him—could it make him more afraid?

"I've got to leave home," he told himself, "to make things easier for Ma. Pa won't get angry so often. I'll join up with an emigrant family heading west . . . to Fort Bridger, maybe. Or maybe to California. I can round up their cattle and drive 'em; and I'll even gather buffalo chips for their fires. Or maybe I'll join the Sioux tribe; they're good to young boys."

He felt the beginnings of homesickness even before he left. Baby Aileen was awake now, making gurgling noises. Too bad she would grow up never knowing she had a big brother, name of Peter. Someday he might come home, man-grown, and surprise her and Ma. Or maybe he'd never come home at all.

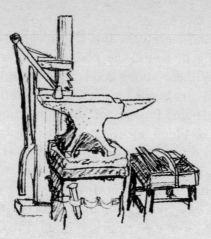

The Fierce God

BY THE time Peter awakened the next morning, his father had already breakfasted and gone. Peter knew it by the peaceful stillness of the house. "Maybe I'm getting like Grandma Lundy," he thought, "sleeping so I can't hear what I don't want to hear."

The teakettle was still humming for him as he pulled on his deerskin shirt over the underwear he had slept in. He would make himself eat to be strong enough for chasing cattle and being a roustabout for Easterners traveling to Oregon. He was glad there was no need for talk as he gulped the cup of strong tea along with the hot johnnycake and molasses. His mother, busy with Aileen, did not notice when he stored some of the johnny-cake in his pocket for an uncertain journey. Nor did she notice his ears redden as he tried to brave himself for a quick good-bye.

"Peter, lad," she said, "turn your back to me. Let's see how good a seamstress I am." Against his shoulders he felt her hands holding up the new woolen shirt, measuring shoulder to shoulder.

"Good!" she said in approval. "If you were to go to the finest tailor back in Syracuse, or even New York City, I doubt you'd get a better fit. Now only the buttons to sew on."

She dismissed him with a pat on his buttocks. It reminded him of the way he slapped a horse he'd grown to love. He hated himself for thinking, "The shirt will be warm to take along. I'll wait for the buttons."

"Oh, Peter," his mother called as he started for the door. "I've a message for you. It's from your father. Tomorrow he's going with some men for our year's supply of salt, and perhaps to hunt along the way. He is counting on you to mind shop while he is gone. And at night," she added, "you're to sleep with his rifle by your side."

• • •

Jethro Lundy's Trading Post & Smithy stood on the direct line of the Overland Stage Route where Rawhide Creek meets up with the north branch of the Platte River. It was built stoutly of timber and adobe. The blacksmith shop occupied half the building, and the trading post—shelved to the ceiling with supplies for the steady westward traffic of wagon trains—took over the other half.

As Peter slow-footed across the road, Dice, his Dalmatian, appeared out of nowhere. The dog was in a bewilderment of joy. The morning was new; his master no longer housebound; and from now until dark they belonged to each other. As plainly as it is given an animal to talk, he said, "You chase me! I've got your ball!" And he began running round and round in widening circles.

Peter's spirits lifted. He joined the chase. From a dead stop he burst into full speed. Round and round they went, Peter chasing Dice, then turnabout. Run! Run! Run! The letter forgotten.

The leave-taking forgotten. Only the good feeling of March wind in his face, and his heart and lungs pumping fast, and his legs moving strong.

Laughing and exhausted at last, he crumbled the johnny-cake that was to have been his journey cake and fed it all to Dice. Then together they headed for the smithy.

Before the open doorway Peter's worry descended like a cloud. He glanced up at his father's sign and was surprised that it wore the same look of yesterday. Somehow he expected the whole world to be different because of a letter written in secret and read in secret by the wrong person.

From within came the clang of hammer on anvil mixed with the strident voices of emigrants wanting to trade their gaunt, tired oxen and horses for Pa's fattened-up and rested ones.

Dice nudged Peter along. He was eager to growl over the hoof parings and bury them before some strange dog snatched them. Once inside the shop Peter suddenly felt the living excitement of the place—horses snorting, mules braying, men swearing and laughing. And towering over all stood Jethro Lundy, full-bearded, with dark curly hair and dark eyes that threw back the glinty sparks of the forge. For long seconds Peter studied his father. He had not dwindled in power or might since the letter. He always seemed to grow between the times that

Peter saw him. "He looks fierce, like God turned angry," Peter thought, "a big, fierce, muscly God, with one finger missing."

God or not, Jethro Lundy was in his element. With one eye on the hired helper fitting shoes to an ox suspended in mid-air, he was at the same time engrossed with the emigrants who had stopped to trade. A man and boy were at the head of a line leading to the counter.

"Mein namen ist Hugo Rummelhoff," the man said. "From Wisconsin we come, by Milwaukee."

The curly-haired god merely nodded, expecting to hear the usual complaints about dusty roads and brackish water and high cost of food. But with Hugo Rummelhoff it was different. He had a deeper trouble.

"Mein boy, Hans," he said, "he's got measles."

Like spooked horses the nearby customers shied away from the boy. But Jethro Lundy remained fixed, ready for whatever.

"Hans, he needs goot warm clothes," Mr. Rummelhoff was saying. "In trade, a steer I give you?" It was more question than statement.

A shudder gripped the slight boy, followed by a fit of coughing.

Mr. Lundy waited, his fingers drumming the counter. Mr. Rummelhoff put a protective arm about his son. "I make it two steer," he said, nodding. "Yah, I make it two."

Mr. Lundy didn't accept or reject the offer. His gaze slid over to the door, to Peter, his eye measuring him against the ailing Hans. "Rummelhoff," he mused, his fingers working in the curly beard, "we got us a pair of skinny weaklings." The hand with the missing finger pointed. "That gangling, yellow-haired boy over yonder is Peter Lundy."

A dozen heads turned to stare.

"Mrs. Lundy coddles him; makes him puny."

"Yah," Mr. Rummelhoff agreed, "womans do tha\
bowed his head in pain. "Mein frau we buried yesterda\
Bitter Creek; she ketched measles, too."

Jethro Lundy appeared not to have heard. "That shirt of
crimson wool," he spoke half to himself, half aloud, "should be
done about now."

"Yah?" the word went up the scale, kindled with hope.

"But, Rummelhoff, two steer, all skin and bone and sore-
footed, ain't worth a handwove shirt. By time I fatten 'em up
for trade I'll have too much money in 'em."

Hugo Rummelhoff dived into his pocket and offered a rope
of tobacco.

Mr. Lundy waved it aside and let his eye travel on to the
next customer.

"Herr Lundy! Herr Lundy!" The voice was desperate now.
"Maybe you like some schnapps? A leetle jug of goot schnapps?"

"Hmmmm . . . mm . . ." Mr. Lundy warmed. His tone became homey as corn mush. "It strikes me your boy needs that
handwove shirt more'n my boy." And all in the same breath he
shouted, "Peter! Whether your ma's finished or not, fetch the
shirt!"

A quiet stretched across the room. In a leap of imagination
Peter saw the boot stamping, crushing the bleeding-heart bush.
Now Pa was hurting his mother again. And he, Peter, was the
cause of it. He answered nothing, but turned and with his dog
walked slowly across the road. He kicked the dirt before him,
wishing with each step that he was kicking his father in the
shins. He wished he could grab that jug, and with his mother's
pistol shoot it full of holes until the schnapps dribbled all over
the dirt in little pellets.

"Ma!" he cried above the whir of the spinning wheel, "my new shirt's being traded for a yoke of ox and a . . ." He stopped. All too soon she would know about the schnapps.

Mrs. Lundy looked out the door left open, and up toward the trading post. "He could have taken your old ones," she said, "but he had to have the new one I made for you. And it still wants a button!" Two tears started down her cheeks.

"Don't cry, Ma. I don't mind about the shirt. It's for a boy my size. He's sick with measles."

Tears still wet on her face, his mother tried to thread a needle, missing three times because of the blurring. "Why, how very nice," she choked as if she had swallowed a fish bone, "how very nice of your father! You must try to understand, Peter, trading is his only joy. And yet," she said in a kind of pride, "he thought of something nice and warm for a sick boy. You do see how generous that was? At least *try* to understand until I give you reason enough."

Peter looked full into his mother's eyes. How could he understand? If she didn't think him man enough to tell him, how could he?

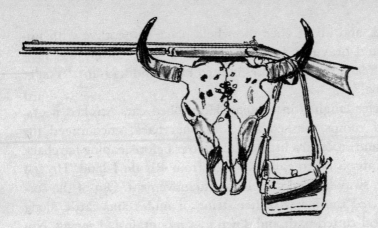

The Shooting Match

THE REST of the day belonged to Peter and Dice. Now no one would bother them. Unless Adam, Pa's helper, came running for Dice to hypnotize a fractious horse.

Meanwhile Peter could get to his own work. In some ways it seemed more important than his father's; maybe even more than Mr. Buchanan's, the brand-new president of the United States. The president's paperwork and his father's trading were one thing; but doctoring lame critters so they could walk again —*that* was prime important.

In exchange for as little as a pound of sugar or a skipple of salt, Jethro Lundy grudgingly accepted horses, oxen, and mules that were too sore-footed and starved from the long, rough journey to go on. These were turned over to Peter because, as his father said, "The dumb understand the dumb."

On this March morning in the year 1857, Peter's patients were bunched up in the corral, looking scraggly and sad . . . until they heard Peter's whistle. Then heads came up, ears

pricked, and all at once the whole place came alive with jos-
tlings and brayings, bawlings and neighings. Gimpy legs hurried to reach the boy. Noses bunted him, chiding him: "You're
late, doc!"

Peter laughed in content. He rubbed ears, stroked necks,
slapped rumps, pushed the bold ones back, encouraged the
timid, and crooned a little critter-patter before leaping bareback
onto Kate, a Narragansett Pacer from Rhode Island. He felt
the big, sway-backed gray leap into movement. Out of the corral she led the helter-skelter string of mules and cattle along
the wheel-rutted path and down to a mountain-fed spring. Not
one animal was tied to the next. Even the newcomers, Mr.
Rummelhoff's steers, limped along with the bunch. Dice, bringing up the rear, was dizzy with importance—running here,
there, everywhere; herding a laggard away from prairie dog
holes, nipping him into line, keeping them all in proper order
head to tail, with no more than an animal's length between.

Turning to look at the caravan winding along behind him,
Peter felt an all-powerful joy. He whistled to a hawk coasting
in the deep sky, and the tune he whistled belonged to his mother's
words:

> Each song has wings;
> It won't stay long.

For the moment he had forgotten last night. Who could
think about a dead letter buried in a box when grass was green-
ing up, and willows fuzzing yellow, and he was both doctor and
nurse to a bunch of brown-eyed creatures who needed him? At
the spring their slurpings and squealings tickled him. Gabriel,
a wise old mule, kept guzzling like a camel long after the others
were through. Suddenly his wary eye caught a herd of buffalo

ranging into view. He gave a roaring snort, and with water still dribbling from his muzzle hurried to join his corral mates.

The humping buffalo browned the landscape. They were drifting toward the spring. In an instant Peter leaped astride Kate, put her to a fast pace, and the entire parade gallumphed for home, leaving the water only a little muddied for the oncoming herd.

Back at the corral Peter went quickly to work, forking hay in small piles here and there to keep the greedy ones from snatching it all. Even so, it was a game of touch tag—Gabriel bunting his way from one mound to the next, with Kate always one pile ahead and the cattle changing places behind. Peter thought, "Even if Pa's trading *is* kind of one-sided, the poor critters are better off here for the good feed and rest before they're traded again." He poured corn mixed with barley into the feed trough, and while the animals shifted and bickered over the choicest morsels, he built a fire of buffalo chips.

Doctoring came next. "Let's warm up the tar now." Peter talked to Dice as to an eager assistant. "It's no wonder their feet are tender; the wheel ruts and sand are worse'n walkin' barefooted on a road of sharp rocks."

He sniffed of the tar melting in a tin can, enjoying the sharp pungency. "Y'see, Dice, we got to swab it on as warm as they can stand it."

He pulled from his pocket a leather mitt and a piece of wood whittled into a spatula. Holding the hot can with his mitt, he headed for Gabriel. Without being told, Dice reached him first, backed him into a shed and sat down facing the mule, staring at him until the animal stood transfixed.

Quietly Peter lifted each foot, cleaned and painted the cracks. Not until the tar cooled to form a gummy coating was the patient released. After the treatment patient and doctor both felt good, and Dice yawned and rolled over on his back, yowling in satisfaction.

Doctoring, Peter concluded, was a splendid business, in spite of knowing that the healed ones would likely be traded off just when he and they became best friends. Daily the faces changed. Where today a Morgan horse grazed, tomorrow there might be a starving mule or a lame ox.

After feet, Peter considered backs next in importance. He examined the few young backs and all the old ones that sagged like hammocks and were rubbed sore by ill-fitting harness or broken saddletrees. He mixed gunpowder with goose grease to make a soothing salve, and he swabbed the tender places. But for Mr. Rummelhoff's oxen he prepared a poultice of flaxseed for the sores where the yoke had rubbed.

And so the day went. A strawed bed to lay for the sow who was ready to farrow. Two hens to set. The chicken house to clean. The long shed to muck out. The manure to trundle to Ma's vegetable patch. He seemed always to be running, carrying his father's lunch bucket from soddy to trading post, running out on the prairie to gather more buffalo chips to build more fires, running even with the yoke laden with two buckets of water over his shoulders, running to crank the grindstone to sharpen Adam's tools.

Emigrant children shyly watched Peter while their fathers were busy at the trading post. Yet no sooner did the shyness wear off than their names were yelled out from rumbling wagon trains and they were sucked into the distance, never to be seen again.

But at sundown this day, seven wagonloads of families with several children apiece pitched camp near the post. Mr. Lundy made an exception and opened the trading post doors after supper. With the help of Adam and Peter he did a brisk business by lantern light. Feeling smug and pleased with the cash in the till, he invited the men to join him in an hour of target practice. He pointed to the moon throwing a path of light across the floor.

"A good night for seeing," he said. "What will it be, gentlemen?" He spoke to the group, but directed his gaze to Whippleby, the wagon boss. "Speak your druthers, gentlemen. Will it be tomahawk throwing? Bow and arrow? Rifle shooting?"

Whippleby, a spare-built man with a crag of a nose, called for rifle shooting. The decision was almost unanimous—except for Sop-tater Jones, who had apparently been sopping something other than gravied potatoes. "I wanna throw a tommyhawk," he giggled. "I wanna throw a tommyhawk."

"Drug him to his wagon!" the boss said.

The man's sons led him away, still giggling, "I wanna throw a tommy . . ."

His Winchester lever-action rifle clinched confidently under his arm, Mr. Lundy led the way out across the road and past the soddy to a spot well behind. The place was worn bald of grass. "Here's our standing mark, gentlemen. It's been trod bare by me and a hull passel of skilled marksmen."

Two dozen or so yards away, under a wild plum tree, an old bench held an assortment of targets—a bleached buffalo skull, a saucer-shaped piece of tin, an antelope horn, and discs of wood of varying sizes.

A tin mug, cut through lengthwise, was anchored to a cottonwood post. What was left of the mug held a candle end.

"Now," said Lundy, "the idea is to kill the flame in the mug without shatterin' the candle."

"Them that has dipped candles themselves," a Scotsman said, "will be careful no to break them, eh, Whippleby?"

"No doot aboot it," Mr. Whippleby mimicked him.

"Well, Peter?" Mr. Lundy barked. "Do I have to hightail it for a new candle? Or will you fetch a half dozen from yer ma?"

The boys gathering about laughed into their hands at the thought of the big, burly trader hightailing anywhere.

Peter ran to the house and returned with the candles and a red-hot ember in an iron pot. With his pocketknife Mr. Lundy scraped out the old, guttered candle in the mug. He now blew on the ember to light the fresh one. Then dripping tallow into the bottom of the mug, he fixed the candle in place. As he waited for the tallow to set, his own face hardened. "Out here, in this wilderness that ain't even a state," he said, "a man has got to take the law into his own hands. Perfecting one's firing skill ain't a thing for fun."

"Ye're damn right, it ain't," the wagon boss agreed. "What with Injuns skulkin' about and road agents thievin'. As to the wager, sir, what's it to be?"

"How about a silver dollar that no man can snuff out the candle with his first shot? Peter! Pass yer hat around." Expertly the father tossed the first dollar over people's heads and into Peter's hat.

Voices clamored.

"I'll throw in."

"And I!"

"Count me in."

"Me, too."

"I winna boast aboot mesel', but I hae three notches a'ready."

The silver dollars piled up as man after man took aim, fired, and missed. Then it was Whippleby's turn. He had insisted on letting his men shoot first. "Probably," Peter thought, "to study how the wind blows."

Whippleby, legs spread apart, raised his rifle. Carefully he took aim, his crag nose making a vast moon shadow across one cheek. The flame wavered ever so lightly. He took aim a second time. His rifle cracked. He doused the candle on his first try.

His two sons started to dance, knees high, hands outstretched for the money. There was much backslapping and noisy laughter and calls to Peter:

"Give Whippleby the money, boy."

"Yeh, give it him. Yer pa can't beat our pa."

"Ain't nobody can beat that."

Whippleby shouted them down. He swaggered over to the candle, twisted what was left of the wick, put a glove on one hand, and lifted the faintly glowing ember out of the pot. Blowing on it until his cheeks belled out like a pumpkin, he relit the candle. "Yer turn, sir," he said, bowing to Peter's father with the faintest edge of a smile.

Everyone stepped back to make way for Mr. Lundy, who deliberately faced around, studying the eyes of his audience, his back to the flame. All at once, as if his life had been threatened, he spun around, pointed, fired. The flame died without sputtering, leaving only the moonshine to show the awe in the men's faces.

In the shoot-out between the two winners, Whippleby's hand trembled visibly. His bullet went wide, struck an owl in a wild plum tree. With a whish and a scattering of ghostly feathers, it fell to earth. It was a pale barn owl, with a white, heart-shaped face. Peter remembered his mother's words after someone had shot his pet rabbit. "You must get used to seeing death," she had said. "We each have to take our turn at life, and then

32

make room for others to follow." Peter wondered if somewhere in the unfathomable night there were a lot of fledgling owls awaiting their feathers. He lighted the candle and bent down to make certain the owl was dead.

Whippleby laughed nervously. "I'll toss it as a target for Trader Lundy," he announced.

Mr. Lundy spoke through tight lips. "When I count ten, toss," he said. "One–two–three–four . . ." The howl of a coyote cut off the next words. The flame wavered as if it had a life of its own. Men and boys stood rooted. Dice scurried to Peter's side. ". . . eight–nine–ten."

The owl went flying into the air, and simultaneously a flash of fire! Then a second flash, like split lightning. The bird burst into fragments of feathers, and the candle flame snuffed out. The smell of gunpowder and melted tallow burned in Peter's nostrils. He felt a son's pride rising in him, but it was a pride mixed with revulsion.

"Have some of my red-eye, Lundy."

"Try my corn juice, Lundy."

"Try my rot-gut, Lundy."

"I'll try 'em all," his father laughed as Peter emptied the silver dollars into his outstretched hands. Then he and Dice left, each trudging slowly to his own shelter.

With a sense of relief Peter reminded himself, "Pa's going away tomorrow. No need to see him in the morning. Or ever again. And next day I'll be going away. Only my leaving'll be forever."

The Halt and the Lame

THE NEXT morning Peter lay dreaming he was an ox hoisted up in a sling, waiting to be shod. And ox-big as he was, he felt himself swaying pleasantly as if by the gentlest breeze, and the breeze had words to it. When he woke, his mother was shaking him, singing for all the world to hear:

> *"Here a star, there a star,*
> *Some lose their way.*
> *Here a mist, and there a mist,*
> *Afterwards—day!"*

Even Grandma Lundy was up early, bright-eyed and happy. She sat at the table, eating like a chipmunk, bending down close to the food, then sitting up straight and nibbling away, her downy whiskers in lively motion. Every now and again she froze in the middle of a chew to listen. "Has he gone?" she whispered.

Peter caught his mother's eye. "Yes," he answered.

With a chippy squeak, Grandma returned to her eating.

Peter's mother was saying, "It seems almost sinful. Here we are enjoying hot biscuits with wild honey and potatoes fried with bacon rind, while Mr. Lundy refused everything but one slice of antelope steak."

"Who's Mr. Lundy?" Grandma asked, her eyes vague.

"Why, he's your son."

"Oh, no, he ain't. Not that big bearded man!" She put down her biscuit and curved her birdlike fingers around Peter's wrist. "This here is my boy."

"Sure, I'm your boy," Peter said. He loved his childlike Grandma painfully well. And not because she had a seemingly inexhaustible supply of peppermints, but because she somehow reminded him of a little wild animal with frightened eyes.

"Of course Peter's your boy!" His mother sent a thank-you smile to Peter. She lifted Aileen onto her lap and nursed her, resting her blond head against the dark ringlets and wrapping the baby's shawl about her own body as well. She seemed to shudder with cold, but Peter knew it for what it was. Worry. He felt the tremble in her voice.

"Peter," she said. "You will try to trade wisely? And keep a careful accounting of everything?"

"Yes, Ma."

"Perhaps then your father will find words of praise."

"I would like that."

"Adam, you know, cannot help you. He's a good and loyal helper, but his mind is that of a six-year-old."

"I know, Ma. He is like a big little brother, but strong as anything."

His mother's face softened. "Go now," she said. "Your animals will be pawing the earth."

• • •

The morning star was still alive in a gray wool sky, but already, off in the distance, wagon trains like white sailboats were parting the grass. Peter would have to work fast—watering, feeding, doctoring—to be ready for the emigrants. Dice flew on ahead to begin the business of morning, bringing in Kate to be bridled. He ran searching for her, dashing into the sheds, then back to the corral, in and out between the legs of the other animals, sniffing for her. At last he caught her trail going away from the spring, not toward it. He dashed back to tell Peter, his forehead wrinkled in concern.

"No need to look anymore," Peter said. "I know where she is." In his mind's eye he saw her pacing along high-headed, and Pa in the saddle, his rifle carried crosswise. They would be half way to the salt lick by now, unless there had been good hunting. He turned the picture off. It was always like this. No sooner would a lame critter be made well and come running to his whistle and nip his shirt in fun and poke her muzzle into his neck than his father swept her out of Peter's life, never to belong to him again.

Dice had no patience for thoughts unless they were his own. He nudged Peter to get busy. And the mule Gabriel butted him from behind, then opened wide his jaws, wheezing out a *"Yeeee-aw! Yee-a-a-aw!"* heavy with urgency.

Peter tousled the shaggy foretop. "So it's you wants to be leader, eh, Gabriel?" He went into the shed and came out with an Indian rug and a rope. "I'll cushion your back with this soft rug and sit high up on your withers, so I can't hurt your saddle sore." He touched his finger to it lightly. "It's beginning to scab over nice."

And so the parade of the halt and the lame clomped out of the corral and hobbled down to the spring.

It was this side of midmorning when Peter, finished with feeding and doctoring, tucked a pencil behind his ear and headed for the smithy. The perfume of it floated out to meet him. There were tar smells and the smells of hoof parings and sweat and leather and pickles and apples, all blended into fragrance.

Inside the cavernous shed, Adam was nailing shoes on a travel-wise horse who accepted the annoyances of trimming and pounding as part of his lot in life. He stood still as a painting of a horse. Dice, seeing that he was not needed, found himself a pool of sunlight and wallowed in its warmth.

Without stopping the rhythm of his work, Adam welcomed Peter with a pleased grin. He was bald as a possum's tail, yet to Peter's constant surprise his arms and chest were hairy. Adam thumbed a sooty finger in the direction of a wagon tire.

Peter examined it. "Ends need welding," he said.

The bald head nodded and the grin widened.

The owner of the wheel came over to Peter. "*You* can weld her?" he asked.

"Little Brother can do 'er!" Adam assured the man.

"Hmm, I guess it's like the books say, 'Skill, not brawn, makes the man.' "

For Peter the day flew. Instead of child's tasks—like sweeping up or filling water kegs—he welded and riveted, helped repair axles and splintered wagon tongues, and stretched wagon tires. And each time that Adam set a shoe and clenched the nails, he presented the rasp to Peter with something akin to pride. "Now, Little Brother, you dast round the toe for me."

At trading, however, Adam threw up his hands. He nodded to Peter to take over as the first customers of the morning trooped in, sunk in despair. Peter whisked off his leather apron, replacing it with one of blue homespun, and hurried over to the coun-

ter, placing both hands, palms down, in an attitude of eager readiness.

The leader, a wiry man with beaver teeth and a voice like the baying of a hound, told his troubles as if Peter could wipe them away like spilled milk. "We got to lighten our load," he bayed. "Three yoke of oxen—good pullers all—taken sick and just up and died."

"We figure they overdrank on the alkali water," the oldest man in the group said.

"Did everything we could for 'em," the leader explained. "Physicked 'em on soap and lard mixed with buttermilk. Oh, Lord, they was sick." He remembered back, running a fingernail between his front teeth as he thought.

"Y'know," the old man added, "dosing seemed to do 'em good at first. Then all to once they fell in their traces, dead, like they'd all been hit by the same bullet."

"Yeh! 'Twas just like that," the others agreed.

"No wonder they worsened," Peter thought, "on soap and lard and buttermilk." He felt sorry about them, sorry for the owners, too. What could he say to show he cared? He leaned forward on the counter, the way he'd seen his father do, and in sudden inspiration spoke his father's words: "The past is a bucket of ashes. Let us improve upon the present. What be your needs now?"

Their needs proved simple indeed. "We're heavy on flour," the leader said. "Iffen you could see your way clear to buy some o' our good wheaten flour, that'd give us ferriage money along the way."

Peter pulled out his father's tabulated list from under the counter and studied it:

Items in low supply	Buy at	Sell at
Dried corn	20¢ per peck	50¢ per peck
Flour	12½¢ per lb.	50¢ per lb.

Items in over supply	Buy at	Sell at
Dried apples	10¢ per lb.	$1.00 per lb.
Coffee	50¢ per lb.	$1.00 per lb.
Vinegar	50¢ per pt.	$1.00 per pt.

Peter reasoned the proposition. "There'll be plenty of time later to make money," he thought, "and since Pa is low on flour and these folks have had such bad luck, why don't I buy all they have at fifty cents and then we'll both come out even?"

With tears of gratefulness the emigrants agreed to his offer. They filed in, bearing the sacks on their shoulders. Peter noted their honesty as they helped him in the weighing and in counting out his money. He felt warm and good when they left, even as he drew a circle around the word "Flour" and arrowed it to the column marked "Over supply."

From then on trading was brisk, and all in Pa's favor. He sold vinegar and molasses, butter and coffee, dried apples and peaches, all at a dollar a pint or a pound, and carefully listed each transaction. He was beginning to see why Pa enjoyed trading. It was a game where both players got what they wanted.

The Buscadero Belt

FROM THE slant of the sun across the doorway Peter knew that wagon trains would soon be circling up for the night and all trading put off until tomorrow. He took off his apron and hung it on the peg alongside his father's. Adam did the same and then shook Peter's hand, clasping it tight in his big, moist grip. "Good night, Little Brother." He was about to climb the ladder into the loft where he lived, and Peter was just thinking how nice it would be if he could run home and bring back a hot supper for Adam, when a clatter outside and a billow of dust inside announced the arrival of a horse and rider.

As the dust settled, Peter saw framed in the doorway a colt standing wet and trembling beside an Indian pony mare, who was blowing as if her lungs were on fire. The man astride the mare let his pin eyes travel quickly about the shop—to the aprons hung up for the night, the fire banked until morning, the food barrels covered. Then he focused on Adam. "You Jethro Lundy?" he asked in a husky voice with urgency in its tone.

Adam clucked in embarrassment and rubbed his bald head. "Aw . . . shucks, sir. I'm just Adam."

"Hey!" the stranger said, jerking up the mare's head and acting suddenly in command. "You're not the *first* Adam, be ye; the one that Eve got into trouble?" He howled at his own joke.

Peter slow-footed around to the foal, who sidled up to his mother. He needed drying off.

The stranger's laughter cut off in the middle. "Boy! Watch that mare! Ye wanna get kilt? Who be you, anyway?"

"I'm Peter Lundy, minding my father's shop."

"Well, ain't I in luck to find me the owner's son! My name's Lefty Slade from Loup Fork. Fact is, I'm *Doctor* Slade." He dismounted and switched reins to his right hand, which was withered to half the size of his left.

He started to shake hands, then changed his mind. He was a long, lanky, ratty-haired man wearing fringed buckskins and a fancy buscadero belt that supported two pistols. His legs bowed out like a basset hound's, and a bowie knife was tucked into his right bootleg. Peter noticed that he carried a third gun in a holster stitched onto his vest. It hung in a slanting position, the barrel of the gun pointing to the rear and the butt tipped forward so the man's good hand could reach for a quick cross-draw. But it was the buscadero belt that the man must prize, decorated with carvings, and with silver rich enough to belong to the long-ago Indians.

Peter noticed, too, that the man acted fidgety and took care not to turn his back to the door. He must have ridden hard, from the looks of the mare and the colt, who now buckled to his knees and fell flat as a doormat near the warmth of the forge.

Suddenly Peter felt uneasy. What did the man want? If it was shoes for the mare, why didn't he say so? Her hoofs were

ragged and needed trimming. She looked to be no more than a three-year-old and probably had gone barefoot all her life. She'd be spooky to shoe. If this man Slade was a doctor, why didn't he take better care of her? He didn't act like a doctor. The few Peter had met were kinder, talked softer, wore great-coats, and didn't scratch under their hats for lice.

The sunlight across the doorway smalled down to a sliver. The stillness grew heavy, made more still by the man's scratching. Peter wished a late wagon train would show up and ask to camp nearby. He almost wished his father would come stomping in.

To make talk he said, "Your mare, sir, she's right young to have a colt, isn't she? Looks to be a real Indian pony."

Slade's eyes made a sweeping search through the open door. "Injuns *give* her to me," he said, with emphasis on the word *give*. "I saved a chief's life. He had cholera and measles."

"At the same time?" Peter asked.

"Yuh! Sick as a pizened dog." The man patted the mare awkwardly, as if the gesture were strange to him. And as he dropped the reins, an ember in the forge flamed and shined up a blue-black scalplock hanging from the mare's bit. Looking at the length of the hair, Peter thought, "Sioux!" and his voice said it without thinking.

Quick as a snake's tongue, Slade's good hand made a cross-draw. He pointed the pistol just above Peter's head, then let it waggle at the glass chimneys, the lanterns. "Yeh, kid. She's Sioux. Like I said," he went on quickly, "they *give* her to me for—for curin' their chief of the smallpox."

"I thought 'twas cholera and measles," Adam broke in.

" 'Twas!" Slade snapped. "And smallpox too. Hadn't been for me, he'd went under. See now why they give me the mare?"

He returned the pistol to its holster.

"*And* her young 'un?" Peter asked.

"Looka here, kid! Didn't no one tell me she's ready to drop a younker. And I got to meet a rich party that needs doctorin' in a hurry, and I can't be slowed down by a sucklin' that's botherin' his ma all the time."

"He ain't now," Adam offered.

"He's too wore out," Peter explained.

"Mare needs shoes," Slade said in a wheedling tone. He put his withered hand on Peter's shoulder. All this while Dice had been sifting the man's smells and now let out a growl, deep in his throat.

"He bite?" Slade asked, removing his hand in a hurry.

"Never bit . . ." Adam said. "Not yet."

The man rolled a cigarette, letting his left hand do all the work. "Can't pay ye, o' course, until I cure this rich man of whatever ails him. So I figger on leavin' this strappin' younker as a pay-down."

Peter looked at the slab-sided foal. He saw him grow to be a colt, then a stallion. Saw him answering to a bare heel, and the two of them traveling free—any road under the sun, under the stars, and over the mountains.

"And when I come back, after curin' this rich man," Slade was saying, "I'll pay ye double for the shoes and collect the colt."

"Supposin' you get kilt?" Adam grinned at the idea.

"If I get kilt, who's to claim the colt? Why, he'd belong forever to Peter Lundy."

"*To me?*" Peter blinked in astonishment and disbelief. How he had misjudged the man! Anyone who'd trade a newborn Indian pony for four shoes at a dollar apiece was a fair man.

He picked up some gunnysacking and went around to the foal, approaching from the side away from the mare. If it was going to be his, then high time he rubbed the little fellow dry.

"Whoa!" The voice turned sharp and cold as a knife blade. "Blow the bellows, boy! Adam! You got shoein' to do! And no monkeyshines."

Acting poky and cool, Adam put on his apron and handed the bellows to Peter. "Git the fire goin', Little Brother."

Dice's tail began to wag. He danced around the mare, making little grunts in his eagerness.

Slade kicked him aside.

"Sir!" Peter cried out. "Don't touch my dog!"

Adam picked up a piece of iron. His grin was gone. "Just leave that dog be."

Slade laughed uneasily. "Meanin' no harm to the cur, I weren't. Only time's short. And ain't nobody—man nor cur—goin' to stop me."

Peter, working the bellows, listened to Slade above the wheezing it made.

"This Injun pony's goin' to be spooky to shoe. Ye can't lift a foot without her rarin' and bitin'." His tone was bossy. "Adam! Soon as I throw this she-devil, you tie her, left front leg to rear right and vicey-versy. Boy! Drop them bellows. I'll get a good head holt and toss her." Laying his rope over her neck, he made his move.

Peter was suddenly unafraid. He shouted with all the voice he had in him. "Wait, Doc! Dice . . ."

The dog needed no command. It was as if he had been waiting all day for this moment. He leaped onto his stool.

Slade's pistol came up menacingly. Was he letting a young pipsqueak tell him what to do? And just when he was ready to shoot overhead to scare the boy, he stopped in bafflement. That dog had mystic powers. Else why was the mare straining toward him? Why were they looking eye to eye? The snorting in her nostrils quieted. There was no sound at all until the foal scrabbled to his feet and went to his mother. She hardly seemed conscious when he began to nurse.

Adam's big hands went to work. As gentle as a woman, he rubbed the mare's leg from knee to fetlock, caressing it, crooning softly. She let him pick up a foot, let him hold it between his knees, let him pare away the ragged and worn wall.

Seconds going by . . . and minutes . . . and Dice holding the mare steady with his gaze. The iron now being fitted to size, now hammered into place; now nails being pounded and clenched. And Peter rounding the toe, rasping it to smoothness, finishing it off. Minutes and more minutes. The left front done. The right front. Left hind. Right hind. And at last Adam straightening up, perspiration dripping from his bald head and down his nose.

"She got bee-utiful feet now," he said.

• • •

It was almost dark when Peter pulled the latch and entered the soddy, leaving an orphaned colt snugged up to Gabriel for comfort. He could still hear the mare neighing to her colt as she was ridden away. He knew he would never forget the sound.

"Vengeance Is Mine"

THAT NIGHT Peter was busy with naming his colt and at the same time braiding a hackamore for him when he heard the sound of hoofbeats. He and his mother exchanged surprised glances: "Pa home a day early? Pray that all's well!"

Soon Peter's name would be shouted to the heavens and he'd have to run out and take off Kate's saddle and bridle, and hang up the underblanket to dry. But his name was not called. Instead, there was a ruckus of animal noises—Gabriel braying a steam-whistle welcome to Kate; and between the *"Yeee-a-a-aws"* came the whinnery squeal of the colt. Peter could picture him gawky-legged, bounding to Kate as his stepmamma, and acting happy as if his small world was almost whole again. Peter felt an enormous pride in the intelligence of his colt.

He wished Pa would call him to explain about the newcomer, and afterward he'd say: "Son! You made a smart trade, taking in this fine colt for four shoes. I'm mighty proud; fact is,

I couldn't of done better." But sometimes Pa insisted on unsaddling his horse himself, "so's it'd be done right."

While Peter waited, he went on braiding and thinking protective thoughts for his foal, and how to put them all in a name. Always before, his animals had come ready-named, like Dice. He thought some of asking his mother to help, but she hadn't seen how delicate and gangly he was. In a way he was glad. It was good to be doing the naming alone. He'd think of something special and grand, something for the colt to grow into. A Spanish name maybe, because all Indian ponies had Spanish blood. What was it he'd read in Ma's treasure chest? His mind drifted back, saw his mother's little-girl printing:

Historick Dates to Remember
First horses landed at Santo Domingo 1493

He mouthed "Santo Domingo." His excitement growing, he divided it into staccato syllables—*San-to Do-min'go.* The Domingo part fascinated him, rang like a melody in his mind. He liked the march of it, as if it held heartbeats or hoofbeats, or maybe drumbeats. He knew that Santo meant saint, but he didn't expect an awkward little colt to be that. He'd shorten it to "San." But the Domingo part he'd never shorten. He could hardly contain his joy at the thought of bringing up a colt with a noble name like San Domingo.

"*Yeh?*" a naggling inner voice asked. "*But do you own him?*"

"Of course I do! Didn't Doc Slade give him to me? To be mine forever . . . ?"

"*If,*" the voice reminded, "*if he never came back.*"

"But Adam said . . ."

"*What'd Adam say?*"

50

"He said, 'That scalplock hanging on the mare's bit weren't a good luck charm. That man's a hoss thief,' he said, 'and hoss thieves just keep a-travelin' till they get kilt.' "

The inner voice persisted. *"But what if the whole Sioux Nation comes after the colt?"*

"Why would they? They've never seen him! He was born after . . ." In sudden alarm Peter thought, "Suppose the colt grows up to look like the mare, and the Sioux see the resemblance?" Peter had no idea what she did look like, underneath all that dried sweat and dust. He'd worry about that later.

Meanwhile his happiness held. For now he'd postpone his running away until the colt was a three-year-old and had its full growth. He drew a deep sigh of relief at the thought of staying. Now he wouldn't feel a prick of guilt every time he thought of his mother's needing him. He'd just keep out of Pa's way, causing as little trouble as possible. . . .

He heard quick bootsteps on the path. The door flew open, and in stomped Jethro Joab Abel Lundy, face flushed, beard parted in a grin of triumph. He hung his rifle on the deer antlers over the mantel and glanced around the room—at Peter busy with his hackamore, at the sleeping Aileen, at Grandma rocking, and Mrs. Lundy hanging a kettle over the fire. He looked from one to the other, silently commanding the braiding and the rocking and the housekeeping to stop. He was like an actor pulling his audience in to him. When he had the full and respectful attention of everyone but Aileen, he announced in stentorian tones: "Aye, sweet is the revenge of an eye for an eye; but why take revenge on a man when you can outwit him?"

Peter listened, wanting to interrupt, wanting to tell about his trading. But who could interrupt Pa, especially when he had a good mood on?

"Oh, Lord," his father was chuckling, "not Thy will . . . but mine . . ." His laughter rang out until it bounced from wall to wall.

Grandma Lundy in her hickory rocker tapped her toe as if in rhythm with some distant music. "That *sounds* like my boy!" she chirped. "Only he don't look like my boy."

Peter's mother added more chips to the fire. It roused and sent warmth to the farthest corners of the room. Soon a plate of cookies was set out, double oatmeal discs filled with wild plum jam, saved for special days like Christmas. Peter wondered what had come over his father to turn him into this happy, booming giant.

With a mouthful of cookie Mr. Lundy was still chuckling. Then he began talking in doublequick time as one recalls a dream, quickly, before it vanishes. He spoke directly to Mrs. Lundy, over and above Peter's head; yet the boy felt that what he said was somehow aimed at him.

"I fathomed a double truth tonight," he said, accepting a cup of tea. "In trading and in life, you might say."

"Yes?" Peter's mother encouraged.

"Number one is: Copy the ways of the hunting cat who sits patient at a mousehole."

Mr. Lundy waited for this to sink in, then went on. "Mr. Cat knows that a whisker spied is not a whole mouse. Nor is a snout. Nor an ear. Nor twin ears. 'Tain't a whole mouse to him till he sees tail and all. Then his hunting instinct gives the order: 'Now! Now's the time!' "

Peter nodded his head in agreement. He remembered a house mouse he'd caught on Christmas Eve when he and Grandma were reciting, " 'Twas the night before Christmas and all through the house, not a creature was stirring, not even a mouse." He'd named it "Not even," and kept it as a pet until it had babies.

All this scurried through his mind while Mr. Lundy took a second cup of tea and helped himself to another cookie. "Patience is the ticket," Mr. Lundy said between bites. "Let a man talk hisself out. More he talks, more he reveals. And more you know, the keener you trade."

Peter's ears were big with listening. He was impatient to tell of his own trading. But Mr. Lundy was holding two fingers in the air, not minding that one was half missing.

"Point number two," he said, "is observe every man who crosses your path. Each man is one of a kind. Some peculiarity, like a red birthmark, or a cleft chin, or eye colors that don't match, or"—he seemed to gloat over one peculiarity not named —"any special mark can trigger your memory to a point in time right outa long ago."

There passed such a look of understanding between his mother and father that Peter felt himself an outsider.

"You met such a man tonight?" Mrs. Lundy asked quietly, her eyes searching her husband's. Peter could feel some deep and hidden meaning in the simple question.

"Aye," said Jethro. "I met him—and I let him go. But first I showed him I could outwit him and outtrade him." He rose and stretched his arms high above his head, as if celebrating a victory. " 'Vengeance is mine,' saith the Lord. Well, I'm satisfied to let the Lord take over."

In the little silence that followed, Aileen awakened and clapped her hands in seeming applause. Then she held up her arms to Mr. Lundy.

A great guffaw of joy escaped him. He swooped the baby into his arms and held her high overhead, watching her fingers reach for the firelight dancing on the ceiling. As he did so, his deerskin jacket fell open, revealing a buscadero belt and an extra holster which hung in a slanting position so a left-handed man could make a cross-draw.

Peter's hand covered his opened mouth. His pa was *not* left-handed.

War Bonnet and Shield

P ETER NEVER did have a chance to tell about San Domingo, but he felt happy that night as he skinned into bed. He was warmed by his father's laughter and for the first time saw justice in his trading—no matter how little he'd given in exchange for the beautiful buscadero belt! Anybody who'd kick a good dog like Dice and who'd run a mare and her colt near to death was a bully and deserved to be trounced, beaten, outfoxed, and pounced on—catwise. Besides, what had the man done to Pa long ago?

Under his breath Peter mumbled his prayers. And this night he slept soundly, feeling closer to his father and happy about the colt.

Before breakfast next morning he was out of the house, hurrying to the corral with a pan of milk, warmed and sweetened with molasses. He couldn't keep from running, spattering the milk over Dice, who stopped to lick his coat and beg for more.

The animals were bunched as usual, oxen chumming together, and horses huddled near Gabriel, who was acting very bossy and possessive, like some stallion-protector guarding his family.

Peter couldn't see Domingo at first, so he leaned over Gabriel's back, and the shock of what he saw caused him to splash milk in every direction. There was the little fellow all right, being vigorously tongue-scrubbed not only by Gabriel but by his real mother!

Peter's voice cracked. "So that's it! Pa traded swaybacked Kate for a young Injun mare, three pistols, and a buscadero belt!" He gave a short, nervous laugh in admiration, almost letting the pan slide from his fingers.

All mouths were eager and pushing for the milk, all except the mare. "And she needs it most," Peter thought. But would she come to him? Or would she remember the blacksmith smell of him, and link him with Slade? He elbowed the others aside and held the offering in his outstretched hand. Instantly, her eyes walled and her tail went up in a loop. Yet she stood rooted. Then her nostrils flared, scenting the sweetness of milk and molasses. She tested the wind for danger. Finding none, she stretched forward, neck reaching, lips questing, and all in a moment her muzzle in the pan. In slobbery draughts she sucked it clean.

Up until now Peter had regarded the pony and her young one as ill-treated creatures in need of peace and each other. But he studied them with a different eye this time. Last evening when Slade rode in, night was closing down and the mare's coat was caked with mud and sweat until he had no idea of the coloring or markings beneath. The colt, too, had looked like nothing but a quivering clay model.

Now in his new ownership Peter sized them up. He saw the mare dozing on three legs, head low, mane and tail a tangle of tumbleburrs. His heart went out to her. The colt, taking advantage of her stillness, wheeled around to nurse. He had been scrubbed so clean by his mother's washcloth of a tongue that his body markings were distinct and curiously beautiful. Pure white he was, with a cluster of red-brown spatters on his rump and along his belly. It was as though he had been caught in a gust of autumn leaves, or as though some Indian paintbrush had created a mystical design on his body.

When the colt looked up, whiskers beaded with milk, the wind blew aside his foretop, revealing more brown—a solid band across his forehead, that continued upward and out until it completely covered both ears, like a bonnet. And underneath his throatlatch and down his chest to the upside-down V made by his legs was a whole shield of brown, edged with flower spatters of this same beautiful color!

Peter was stunned. He had seen Chief Red Cloud in ceremonial dress ride a white stallion with a browband of red, and a shield of red, and flower clusters of red. He had thought the designs were painted on for special occasions, like warring or rain-making. But all the time they were real! He was tempted to lick his finger and rub it across Domingo's markings to make sure the pattern did not come off, but the mare's tongue had already made sure.

He wondered: If she too were scrubbed clean, would she be wearing a war bonnet and shield? He ran to the well and pulled up a bucket of precious water. It would not be wasted. Pa would see what a special pair stood in his corral.

Peter's hand went quietly along the mare's neck, wiping away all fear. She leaned in his direction, barely turning her head at the sound of light footfalls.

"Peter?" His mother had stepped up so that not even the colt had shied. "You forgot your breakfast," she said, "but who wouldn't with a brand-new colt to care for?"

"*And* its ma!" Peter said. He was busy dipping his fingers in the water, removing mud and brambles from the mare's mane. He lifted her forelock and washed the place underneath where there might be a brown band. He rubbed behind one of her ears where she couldn't possibly reach to scratch herself, and with his other hand trembling in eagerness he washed away, very gingerly, the sweat and the mud. His heart missed a beat.

"Ma!" he whispered in awe. "Look, Ma. She wears a war bonnet . . . just like the colt's!"

All around them Gabriel and the others formed a circle of watchers.

Mrs. Lundy's laughter rang out. "Why, it does look like a bonnet!" she exclaimed. "The kind horses wear in fly time."

"Only hers and the colt's are grown on, permanent!"

"They are indeed. But, Peter, how did she find her way back here? Did she run away from Doctor Slade?"

Peter smiled at his own reasoning. "Why, Pa took her in trade," he said, with a touch of pride for his father.

"In trade for what?"

"For Kate, the Narragansett Pacer."

Mrs. Lundy sighed happily. "And now a little family is back together again. Oh, Peter, it's just like a storybook."

She reached into the basket over her arm and took out two biscuits and a piece of dried meat. "You've no time now for these," she said, tucking the biscuits into his pocket, "but I won't leave until you are chewing like a cow with her cud."

Peter tore off a piece of jerky and poked it into his mouth. He could keep on working while he chewed.

"Now I must get back to Aileen and Grandma," his mother said, with an uneasy glance toward the house.

"Wait, Ma!"

"What is it, Peter?"

"Please, will you name her? I named the colt San Domingo and I was figgerin' to name his ma Emily after you, but then how'd you know if Pa was yelling for you or her?"

"That *would* be confusing," his mother agreed.

The colt made his way toward Mrs. Lundy's straw basket, started to lip it. The mare darted between and nipped him away. "Nosy colts get bit," she told him with her strong incisors.

"Think quick, Ma! She should have a new name right away so she forgets her Indian one."

"Mmmm . . ." To help her thinking, Mrs. Lundy began humming a few bars of "Santa Lucia."

"Ma!" Peter shouted. "That will do fine."

"What will?"

"Loo-chee-ah." His voice softened as he spun out the familiar name. "Loo-chee-ah," he repeated again.

Even with a mouthful of jerky, it sounded beautiful.

• • •

When his mother left, Peter went back to hand-washing the mare . . . slowly, carefully . . . and with much palaver in as low and deep tones as he could muster. He tried out all the Indian words he remembered. "*Chikala! Chikala!* (Little one)," he was muttering when his father spun him about.

There was a look on Mr. Lundy's face that Peter knew. Disgust. Contempt. He was brandishing a white card, and his knuckles matched the whiteness. Even with the card upside down, Peter could make out the line: *Flour, Buy at 12½¢, Sell at 50¢.*

His name was called. "Pe-*ter!*" The *r* rumbled like thunder, and the voice was a quirt, lashing about his ears.

Domingo let out a surprised squeak and sprang to Lucia's side, upsetting the pail of water over Mr. Lundy's boots. Quickly Gabriel and the others sidestepped the water. Dice, his tail tucked under, hid himself in Peter's shadow.

A cold perspiration came out over Peter's body. He felt like a creature roped, and the rope being pulled hard and slow, tightening about his throat. He heard the water from the pail gurgling into the parched earth. His throat felt parched, too. He forced himself to look up into the glowering face that was mostly beard and brow. Only the eyes alive, but cold, like the eyes of the glass cat on the hearth when the fire is gone.

Again the whip-sound of his name. "Pe-*ter!*"

"Yes?" A voice so small the wind almost blew it away.

"You stood in my place at the trading counter yesterday."

"Yes, s-sir."

"You ever see this list?" Mr. Lundy waved the card.

"Y-yes."

The colt made a whuffing sound and began suckling his mother. Seeking comfort, Peter stole a look at them.

Mr. Lundy stamped his wet boots. "To blazes with that consarn colt! He'll be a troublemaker 'til he's gone."

" *'Til he's gone?* Pa, he's mine! Doctor Slade gave him to me."

"*Doctor* Slade!" A laugh that was not a laugh came on strong. Mr. Lundy's concern went back to the card. He pointed to the line. "Ever hear of the staff o' life?"

"Yes, sir."

"What is it? Speak up!"

"Bread."

"What's it made of?"

"Flour."

"When I buy flour, what do I pay per pound?"

"Twelve and a half cents, sir."

"And when I sell?"

"Fifty cents."

Now the anger mounting. "How many pounds did you buy yesterday?"

"A hundred and thirty pounds."

"And what did you pay the man?"

The white teeth in the bushy beard terrified Peter. He pressed his leg against the warmth of Dice. "Fifty cents a pound," he answered.

"And that makes my profit what?"

A dead weight of silence, broken by two small spoken syllables. "Nothing."

"Nothing!" The tone was icy cold now. "N-o-t-h-i-n-g. And that spells Peter Lundy. Ah . . ."

Peter braced himself for the hail of words.

"Ah, you've time enough for reading at your mother's side. Yellow hair and yellow hair together—reading, laughing. But figures?" His thumb closed over his fist and clenched the card into a wad. "What is twelve and a half from fifty?" he spat out the question.

Peter guessed wildly. "Thirty-six and a half, sir?"

"Oh, Emily," the lion roared, "see what you've done to this boy!"

Peter looked around, but his mother was nowhere near.

Arms upraised, Mr. Lundy was crying to the heavens: "Emily! How will the boy ever fend for himself if he can't do simple arithmetic? You are making a milksop of him!"

Into the awesome quiet that followed, Gabriel let out a *"Hee-haw"* to match Mr. Lundy's howling.

The man turned on his heel as if he had lost the argument.

"I Hear Eyes..."

LONG PAST noon Peter sought out his mother, wondering if she had suffered because of his blundering. As he lifted the latch and peered in, he found her and Grandma Lundy stringing big wooden beads. They looked up quickly, then smiled, relieved that it was only he who had caught them in such foolishness.

With a curve of her fingers Grandma summoned Peter close. Her eyes were bird bright. "I hears you got the purtiest· suckling colt. *And* its mamma!"

Peter's misery eased. He nodded.

"I got a hankerin' to see the both of 'em," Grandma went on. "Now if you was to ride by the door, I'd stir my old bones outen this rocker and come take a look."

"It's a fine idea, Peter," his mother said. "This is one of Grandma's good days."

"And you can make it even better, lad. Only be quick about it afore I doze off. Then the devil hisself couldn't rouse me."

Peter glanced sidelong at his mother. If she had been caught in Pa's storming, she was hiding it well. He would try, too. It was better this way.

"Aileen has never seen a baby colt," she was saying. "With Domingo's spotted markings, she'll probably think he's a dog like Dice."

Revived in spirit, Peter ran out to the saddling shed, coaxing Lucia inside with a handful of corn. While she was busy grinding it into mush, he threw an Indian rug over her back. "As long as you're Indian broke," he told her, "we won't need a saddle nor any mean old bit."

He slipped a hackamore over her nose, attaching a hair rope for the reins. Then he sprang onto her back and headed across the road to the house.

Lucia, content with the lightness of her load and the absence of metal restraints, stepped out briskly, her colt kicking and capering alongside. Dice, not to be outdone, leaped in ten-foot bounds. Grandma was already in the doorway, peering out from the folds of her shawl like a somber turtle. Peter's mother steadied her with one hand while with the other she held Baby Aileen on her shoulder.

Peter paraded Lucia in and out among imaginary barrels, yelling and whooping until his audience caught the flame of his excitement. Aileen shouted in glee, clapping her pat-a-cake with vigor, and Grandma threw out her hands in such rapture she almost toppled.

"Why, they're identical!" Mrs. Lundy said. "Marking and coloring both."

Around and around in a small circle Peter rode. Then he pulled up at the doorstep so everyone could have a close view. Lucia spraddled her legs ever so slightly and the foal rushed to her side. He bunted her in fierce play, then nuzzled up to nurse. All in an instant his flappy tail was keeping time to the suckly noises he made.

The audience in the doorway watched in silence. When at last Domingo had drunk his fill, Grandma threw Peter a kiss and disappeared within.

Peter turned to his mother. "I'd like to ride Lucia to the spring," he said. "She could paw and drink and have some fun."

"Yes!" his mother agreed. "She probably could use a bit of a holiday from that hungry baby of hers."

"You really think so, Ma?"

"I most certainly do. He'll beller some, left behind. But it's the best way to begin his weaning. He'll learn to give up his mother gradually." Then as an afterthought she added, "But short gallops only, Peter. Remember, she's pretty young to be a mother."

When Peter heard the high whinkering of San Domingo as he and the mare left the corral, he almost mistrusted his mother's advice. The crossfire of squealing and neighing lasted until they were well out on the plain, traveling in the path made by iron-rimmed tires and countless feet of emigrants and beasts of burden. With the wind in Lucia's face, the cries of Domingo thinned out and were silenced. A wagon train approached with two colts running free. One of them kited in Lucia's direction. She hesitated. Then, realizing it was not her youngster, she stepped out confidently, almost larking her way along.

Peter found himself whistling. Riding an Indian pony was a different feeling from riding Kate, the pacer. Much as he loved Kate, she had a funny side motion when she walked, a kind of wriggle. Pa called her a side-wheeler. But Lucia's step was all forward going, and so smooth he felt suspended somewhere between earth and sky.

Maybe now was the time to keep on going and never come back. Who cared for arithmetic anyway? What matter the cost of flour? Freedom was the staff of life, not bread. If he just kept loping along like this, away to the ridged mountains, and over and beyond, his father could never find him, never taunt him, never again say, "Yellow head to yellow head laughing." And his mother would never again be hurt because of him. Dice, racing on ahead, seemed to like the idea.

They came to the spring, and Peter's dreaming was so deep he didn't notice the fresh tracks around it. Lucia's drinking and plashing were pleasant to his ears.

He did not head back home. The early afternoon sun was warm on his back, and warm on the mare so that the smell of her was good in his nostrils. "It will be hard on little Domingo," he thought. "He'll have to grow up without a mother. But Ma'll take extra care of him because of grieving for me. And Pa'll miss Dice when it comes to shoein' the frisky ones. He might even miss me and call out in his sleep, 'Pe-*ter!* Pe-*ter!* Come home!' "

Still busy with his dream, Peter rode on. He'd make out just fine. A person could live for years on berries and fish. And Dice could eat jerky. In time he'd grow rich from rounding up stray cattle and horses lost by the emigrants. As for Lucia, she'd fatten on just buffalo grass.

Peter flicked his rope end at a fly that had landed on her neck. Maybe it'd be better to join up with just one train, instead of going from one to another. That way, it'd be more homey.

Or maybe, to earn a heap of money, he'd work for the Majors and Waddell Express Company. With a pocketful of dollars, he'd go back to his father and buy Domingo outright. Any moment now one of their freighters would be coming along, looking for an extra hand. And soon he'd be riding ahead, scouting for Indians and buffalo and outlaws. And when he wasn't scouting, he'd take the driver's place, sitting up on the box, driving the six-horse hitch. Lucia'd be the leader because theirs had just broken a leg and the driver, with tears streaming down his face, had had to shoot him.

But there was no dust cloud in the distance announcing the approach of a stage, or anything at all. There was just grass and wind and sky, without even a bird coasting in it. Nor a cloud. Except along the horizon where tufts of feathers scudded along like the wool-dust Ma swept up every day and threw into the fire.

Peter felt a sudden loneliness as he passed an abandoned wagon, tongue and all wheels missing, and the skull of a cow lying near with new grass growing through the holes where the eyes had been.

He whistled for Dice to stay close.

"Funny," he thought, "with millions of buffalo and wild horses, and thousands of wagon trains crisscrossing the plains, there's no one but us." He thought of home. Ma would be slicing potatoes about now, and Aileen looking for him to give her a piggyback ride. With his eyes closed, he tried a halfhearted laugh. "I swear," he said to the empty land, "more'n more I mind me of Grandma, a-rockin' and rockin' and on her bad days keening: 'I hear eyes a-lookin' at me. I hear eyes . . .'"

Alert now, he opened his eyes and swiveled his head like

an owl's. And still there was only emptiness—until—far along the skyline in the purling clouds he saw,' or thought he saw, a quiver of movement. It was no more than the shimmer of heat on an August afternoon. But here it was only spring! It must be something alive! Mustangs, likely. In wild exuberance he galloped in their direction. Lucia seemed eager to meet them head on. Her new shoes drummed the earth. The grasses parted to her touch. Peter laughed. He was Moses crossing the Red Sea!

The movement in the cloud stilled. "If it's Indians hiding," Peter thought, "they'll know me and come riding out . . . unless they're a faraway tribe."

He heard them before he saw them. Heard their piercing yells, heard arrows singing past him and a rifle ball whining. He reined in, shouting, "*Kola washté! Kola washté!* (Me friend!)"

His voice was lost in their hollering. Only four Indians coming on, but sounding like a nation. He tried sign language, thrusting his right hand to his heart; then guiding Lucia with his knees, he threw both arms forward, forefingers held tight together in friendship. But the Indians swept on, coming closer, brandishing lances and bows. One waggled a rusty rifle.

Where to hide? Which way to go? In all the vast prairie he was the target. Instinctively he wheeled toward home. Lucia broke out in sweat. She was headed back to her youngster! Dice, yipping and yawping, led the way.

The world was all noise and hissing arrows, and the blood roaring in his head, and Indians gone crazy. If only they'd take a direct course; but they came at him in half-circles, first on one side then the other, each time nearer and nearer until they were ahead and he tailing; and now the four of them dashing at him, shooting their arrows, aiming at the earth in front of him, throwing clods of dirt in Lucia's face, trying to stop her. Suddenly Peter knew. They took him for a horse thief! They were after Lucia!

Peter skinned off his shirt, waving it as a peace sign. A young warrior with red horseshoes painted on his face swung alongside, speared Peter's shirt into the air, grinning and waving it on high. He was riding broadside of Peter, and now careened sharply in front of him. The mare reared to miss him, but one of her forefeet raked the Indian's thigh, drawing a ribbon of blood. Laughing, the warrior wiped the crimson on his hand and smeared it over his face. Then he slid off his horse and grabbed Lucia's rope, ripping it out of Peter's hands and jerking him to the ground.

The other three Indians surrounded Peter. They wore their hair in double braids down their backs. Peter felt a moment of hope. They were Sioux! The Sioux were his friends!

"How!" he said in a thin voice. "How!" he tried again, deeper this time, while Dice's growl grew strong and threatening until a whack with the rifle brought a whimper of pain and shame. Then more growling, fiercer than before, and Peter trying to think fast before they killed Dice. "Go home, Dice! Go home!" he shouted.

Three of the Indians were arguing among themselves, even as they came at him, lances prodding. Peter caught the word *"Péhin,"* meaning "hair." And then fiendish laughter and the youngest Indian saying, *"Péhin shokala,"* meaning "thick hair."

Peter froze. He'd seen a scalped man. He remembered the throb of blood beating in the skull, marking the count of the heartbeats. Peter would rather die.

His eyes sought the big Indian with the rifle, asking in sign language to be shot instead of scalped. The man understood, but his powder was gone. He reached into his quiver, pulling out an arrow. The others were silencing Dice with blows, now prodding Peter with their lances, turning him around and around until he was dizzy. They were planning to shoot him in the back!

Suddenly he heard his own voice, big in his throat, and he was commanding, "*Makpia Luta tipi ichuwo!* (Take me to Red Cloud's tepee!) *Kolapi washté!* (We good friends!)"

The Indians stopped their shouting. Their eyes hunted one another's. The Indian with the rifle motioned Horseshoe Face to give Lucia's rope back to Peter, motioned Peter to put his shirt on and climb aboard.

In single file, with Peter in the middle and Dice limping in the rear, they took off toward the camp of Red Cloud.

"Him Damn Lucky"

INSIDE HIS tepee Red Cloud, chief of the Sioux Nation, sat cross-legged on his throne of buffalo robes. His hair was pierced by a single eagle's feather. Rattlesnake tails dangled from his ears, and bear claws circled pendants in his ears, and a string of grizzly-bear claws circled his neck. For clothing he wore only leggings and a breechclout; yet he was resplendent in the magnificence of his shoulders, the depth of his chest, the glossy sheen of the blue-black braids. Dignity marked his cold face.

Peter moved slowly toward him, frightened when the firm lips did not move. He tried a timid "How."

The jaw muscles tightened. There was no familiar twinkle in the dark eyes. No flashing of white teeth. He was not the same Indian who tossed Aileen into the air, and shook hands with Ma and ate her rice pudding, saying, "Damn good!" and "More sugar, thanks."

Outside, Peter heard dogs barking and men and children shouting, but all was stillness within the tepee. The only sounds

73

came from a half coyote bitch licking a ragged gash on Dice's leg. The silence was suffocating; it was like being caught in quicksand, being sucked down, down, down until even his lungs were squeezed of air. He said a quick prayer under his breath, felt it answered when Red Cloud stirred, pointing an outstretched arm toward Lucia, who was just visible beyond the opening of the tepee. Then the big hand scalped Peter in sign language, and the gruff voice said: "Red Cloud make war! Kill many!" Both arms shot wide, as though slaughtering the whole world. "Who steal Injun pony? You tell Red Cloud and we no make war. Maybe."

Peter let out his breath and gulped for more. The memory of Lefty Slade came sharp and clear. Even the ratty smell of him. Peter thought of Pa's advice: Observe how each man is one of a kind. Doc Slade would be easy to describe, but it would mean the man's almost certain death . . . unless he and old Kate had made it over the mountains to Oregon. Peter weighed one life against many. There was no choice.

A straggle of children came into the tepee, returning an armful of almost grown pups to the bitch. One pup was biting at fleas. Peter was suddenly reminded of Lefty's lice. He shoved an imaginary hat back on his head and scratched at imaginary lice to gain thinking time. Where should he begin? With the man's withered hand? With his firearms?

As the scratching went on, the boys were tittering behind their hands. Lice were something they understood. But there was neither amusement nor friendliness in Red Cloud's eyes. His face was sealed as if with wax.

Peter's mind went hopping from lice to guns to the crippled hand. He decided to show the guns first. He went into pantomime, wrapping the buscadero belt low about his hips, keeping his thumbs and middle fingers inches apart, showing how very wide the belt was. After tying the make-believe thongs securely, he patted the two guns, one on either hip. Next he made as if he were slipping a pistol into a holster pocket fastened onto a vest, chest high—not over his heart but to the right.

Red Cloud leaned forward, eyes squinted in concentration as Peter began acting out the withered hand. With his left hand he now pointed to his right hand, which he slowly drew

up into his right sleeve so that only the fingers showed, dangling puny and helpless. Then in a lightning-quick motion his strong left hand made a cross-draw and shot Red Cloud dead!

There was total silence. For a terrible instant Peter's stomach sickened at his daring. Then, slowly, the eagle feather in Red Cloud's hair waggled up and down. He nodded at the clue, and at long last the waxen face melted into a slow grin of understanding.

"Him road agent," Red Cloud said, strangling the man with both hands. Then his eyes went kindly. "*Chante ohitika!*" he said, praising Peter for his brave heart. He called to his squaw, whose wrinkled face poked into the tepee. "*Wota,*" he said to her. He sawed himself in half with his thumb and pointed to Peter.

"Ah, Yellow Hair hun-ger-y," the squaw said, grinning at the sign talk.

With the grace of an antelope, Red Cloud bounded to his feet and went out to the mare. He studied her, felt her legs, admired her new shoes. "*Washté!* (Good!)" he said.

Then he noticed her full milk bag and the drops of milk on the ground. He looked straight at Peter.

Peter placed his hand over his heart. "Me, I have colt." He crossed his forearms, forefingers pointing: "Trade. Me trade," and he pointed to Lucia's new shoes. "Me give shoes for colt." He clasped his left forefinger in his right fist and held it firmly. "Me keep colt?" he asked hopefully.

Red Cloud's eyes looked beyond Peter, looked past Horseshoe Face and the three young warriors who stood waiting, past the wagons and the children to some other time and place. To Peter he suddenly seemed a wise judge or a prophet out of the Bible. He wondered how this fatherly person could have killed the eighty-one men in the massacre at Fort Kearney. "They must have someway deserved it," he thought.

At last Red Cloud came back to the here and now. He crossed his arms, ready to trade. *"Washté!"* he said again. "You keep colt. She," he said, stroking Lucia's neck, "she make many more for me. Many as fingers of Red Cloud's hands." And he ticked them off on his ten fingers.

He disappeared into the tepee and returned with his squaw carrying a blue jug. While Red Cloud held Lucia still, the squaw deftly milked her until the bag was no longer swollen. To Peter's open-mouthed amazement, she presented the jug to Red Cloud, who drank noisily, smacking his lips with pleasure.

Then Peter and Red Cloud sat down to *wota,* consisting of hot pemmican cakes and a bitter brew that Peter managed to swallow. "No wonder Red Cloud found Lucia's milk so tasty," he thought.

The huddled puppies were asleep, and Peter was wondering where he would sleep this night when Red Cloud arose, made him a present of the blue jug still encrusted with Lucia's milk, and his rattlesnake earrings.

"For Mama," he said, "and baby 'Leen."

Peter thanked him in his best Sioux. *"Pilamayelo!* (Oh, thank you!) *Pilamayelo!"*

Red Cloud was pleased. "Yellow Hair gude boy," he said. He clapped his hands, summoning the four braves to escort Peter home.

Riding double behind Horseshoe Face, Peter kept sluing around, first to make sure that Dice was keeping up, then looking backward, to watch Lucia until she was lost in distance. Horseshoe Face reached around and held Peter's leg still. "Yellow Hair still have yellow hair!" he said. "Him damn lucky."

It was getting on toward evening when Peter walked into the house carrying the blue jug. Mrs. Lundy, in the middle of supper preparations, ran to him in relief. For a moment she held Peter close and whispered: "I warmed milk for Domingo." Then quickly she turned to her skillet, flipping the sliced potatoes that were browned on one side.

After supper Peter acted out his meeting with Red Cloud, doing the pantomime all over again, playing the roles of both Lefty Slade and Red Cloud.

Her cheeks pink with pride, his mother applauded heartily. And Grandma said, "What's wrong with your pore dangly arm?" His father's reaction took him by surprise, though afterward he wondered why it should. "Least you could've done," Mr. Lundy grunted, "was make a decent trade! Who but Peter Lundy would give away an Injun-gentled three-year-old mare for an untried suckling? You should've brought home furs— ermine and fox and white wolf. Eh, Emily?"

The mother dared to say, "He made the best trade of all. *His* life for the mare."

"Injun Gentled"

DOMINGO! THAT little scrap of Injun royalty was a challenge, a nuisance, and a joy. In those first days with the orphaned colt Peter thought, "As long as he needs me for a mother and a teacher, I'll be here. I'll put up with Pa as something like mosquitoes or locusts or dust."

But gradually—so gradually that Peter wasn't aware when it happened—the tables turned. It was Peter who needed Domingo! For the first time since he had come upon the hidden letter, he felt a sense of security in living under his father's roof. He possessed a colt of promise, and without a word his father seemed to admit as much. Now the colt was twice his. First, given him by that outlaw Slade, and then by Red Cloud.

Strangely, Mr. Lundy began to leave the boy alone. Of course, he made sure that Peter took care of doctoring the motley collection of animals, and that he did his house chores, too, but the between-times belonged to Peter. It was as though man and boy were glad to be freed of each other.

Right from the start of bringing up Domingo, Peter couldn't remember ever having been so happy. At first the foal would wobble with the wind—head up, nostrils and lips questing for his mother. He found Peter instead. Peter offering a finger dipped in milk and molasses. Peter letting him suck what flavor he could get. Then the finger submerged deep in the bowl, and the colt having to bury his muzzle in the milk to find it. Before the week was out, finger licking was colty foolishness. Now Domingo nearly upset the pan in his eagerness to slobber up the warm goodness. And so the transition from suckling to weanling took as naturally as night going into morning.

After the meeting in Red Cloud's tepee, Peter joined the Sioux Nation in his mind. He let his hair grow long, until he could wear it down his back in two braids.

"Me albino Sioux," he laughingly told his mother.

And he copied their way of horse talk. He remembered how Red Cloud had uttered deep-chested sounds when he took hold of Lucia's rope, and how she had stood very still, ears pricked toward him to listen. The words sounded like *"Hoh, hoh, Chikala, hoh, hoh."*

When Peter tried to mimic the deep pitch of Red Cloud's voice, his *"hoh-hohs"* came out in thin whuffs. Yet Domingo listened intently, like some schoolboy hungry for learning. He seemed to regard Peter with respect, amounting to hero worship. If danger threatened—coyotes skulking close to the corral or wolves on the prowl for colt-meat—he bugled for Peter. Whatever the danger, it melted away with the boy's nearness. And so the invisible tie-rope between them tightened and strengthened.

Day by day, Peter touched Domingo—starting his fingers along the colt's neck, touching the crest, feeling the straight line of the back where someday he would be sitting, and the belly where his legs would be held close, and the place where his heel would nudge Domingo when they both wanted to gallop. And with the flat of his hand he would touch the flanks, each red flower cluster. And his fingers would lift the forelock, tracing the bonnet of red hairs going up and over each ear.

With combing fingers he separated the hairs of mane and tail. And when Domingo was sleepy, he would often cup the whiskery chin in his palm.

As time wore on, he practiced sliding gentle hands down the forelegs, and later down the ticklish hind legs. And he peered into the colt's mouth, his thumb resting on the bar of gum where there would never be teeth, where sometime a rope would lie, and sometime the bit.

Weeks passed. And months. And then an arm slid over the colt's back, coming down and around his barrel, tightening as if it were a cinch; and then one day the boy's body hoisting itself up, draping itself across Domingo's back like an inert thing, a rag doll, arms dangling down on one side, legs on the other; a rag doll lying there still while Domingo pranced about, testing whether the limp thing would slide off. But instead, strong hands were grabbing strands of mane, and the rag doll was up, legs forking apart, thighs tightening against his barrel. The rag doll: a horseman astride! And at last Peter riding around the corral. He was riding! Riding! Riding! And his voice bursting in his lungs: "He's *Injun* gentled, *Injun* gentled! Oh, Ma! Come and look!"

• • •

Riding often and everywhere gave Peter a feeling of wild freedom, freedom from the critical eye of his father. It was a timeless time of pure joy. With no clock but the heat of the sun and the length of his shadow, Peter lived like an Indian boy with pony and dog for company. At nooning he swam in Rawhide Creek, sousing his head in the water, cooling and freshening himself, swimming and winking at solemn-eyed

frogs who blinked back. Dice, who hated water, played with Domingo. One day Dice grabbed the lead rope in his teeth and ran the colt in circles.

Peter shot out of the water, intending to rescue Domingo. But he stopped short. Domingo was following Dice in high spirits. Even with the rope gone slack, he was rounding the curves, galloping the straightaways, playing follow-the-leader as if this were an old, familiar game. It was Dice who wore out first. With fine discipline he brought Domingo back to the starting point and ground-tied him. Then he trotted over, grinning, to Peter with a see-what-I-did look.

After his swim, Peter fell down on the bank, letting wind and sun blow and bake him dry. It was fun lying on his back, listening to a magpie chattering, and seeing for the first time that the white belly of Domingo was not white, but green, reflecting light from the grass into the white shadow. Someday he would paint a picture of Domingo with a greenish belly, and only Ma would believe it. On these carefree afternoons boy and pony, too, often fell asleep listening to the murmur of the creek while Dice whiskered around for rabbits or prairie chickens.

There was no need for worry. The whole Sioux Nation seemed to know that Yellow Hair rode a white stallion who wore a natural red war bonnet. Whenever Peter and Domingo met a lone Indian, or a party, teeth flashed in recognition and hands raised in "How!" Even the Arapahos and the Cheyennes let the boy and his horse alone. And so the days and weeks ran together.

One early evening when Peter returned to the house, his braids still wet with the day's swim, his mother said, "I'm sending off a letter to your uncle today."

A look of startlement crossed Peter's face. Did Ma suspect that he had found and read her long-ago letter? He turned his face away from her and tried to make his tone casual. "To my Uncle Peter in Syracuse?" he asked.

"Yes," she said, coming to poke the fire and sending up a shower of sparks. She spun Peter around, smiling at him, puzzled. "Peter! Don't you want to *know* what I told him?"

Peter was not sure. Maybe what happened to Pa long ago was best forgotten. Or maybe this was a new letter, all fresh and different. "Yes, I want to know," he said, trying to put confidence into his words.

His mother melted a dab of beeswax for sealing her letter. She watched it cool and set before answering. Then she said, "I wrote him that little Domingo had grown as important to you as you and Aileen are to me. Yes," she said, "I went so far as to say that life might never be so happy for you again."

Peter felt a truth in Ma's words. Sometimes his happiness with San Domingo almost frightened him. It seemed too great to keep.

Part II. The TRANSIT

The Whirling Sky

HIS NAME is Peter Lundy and he is fourteen, and he and his stallion are familiar sights on the plains as far west as Fort Laramie, and even beyond. Homesteaders and cattlemen emigrating to the fertile valleys of the Northwest were constantly on the alert for boys like Peter to help round up lost stragglers, or save horses and cattle made crazy by a buffalo stampede. Wagon bosses counted themselves lucky when Peter and Domingo pitched in with their own herders, riding hell-bent to turn the pounding tide of buffalo away from the line of travel.

After a day of eating dust and not much else, Peter was often rewarded with nothing more than a hand laid kindly on his shoulder and a heartfelt thank-you. But sometimes the pay was a shiny gold piece, or a steer to keep; and on that day Peter could face his father.

Around campfires at night mountain men and miners, bull-whackers and mule skinners, freighters and trappers spoke of the skinny kid with yellow braids and the odd-marked young stallion who flew over the land at the speed of an antelope. "Seems like," they said, "neither one ain't afeared of nothing."

But on the sultry afternoon of July 14, 1859, Peter and Domingo both felt fear. The day began with the sun rising in a flood of crimson. Peter had been sent early by his father to find a team of oxen that had strayed in the night. By the time he had rounded them up, the sun was hot and brassy overhead.

On impulse, he angled Domingo away from the trading post, up Rawhide Creek, toward his swimming hole. He felt a twinge of guilt at not stopping for Dice; but the dog was busy at the shop hypnotizing, one by one, a string of fresh-broke Army horses getting their first set of shoes. Resolutely Peter went on, pulled by the thought of slithering into the cool water, paddling among the chub and sauger fish.

His swimming hole seemed especially friendly today, the willows dipping their fingers in and out of the water, beckoning him to "come on in—the water's fine."

Almost instantly Peter forgot the heat and dust. He dived in, making so big a splash that minnows darted in all directions. For a long time he wallowed in the water. He was like a person desert-dried, thirsting and parched, every pore crying out for water. He sousled his head in the wetness, making fierce noises, then bounced out, trying, unsuccessfully, to balance on a bobbing log. And then right back in again, until laughing in exhaustion he lay on his back, floating quietly with the small current, watching white clouds floating too. The clouds looked good enough to spoon up and let melt in his mouth—like Ma's snow pudding or her whipped syllabub. He could hear Domingo tearing the bunchgrass and sneezing bugs away. Deep in content, Peter closed his eyes and dozed.

When next he looked up, the clouds were smaller, darker, closer to earth, and racing along in a topsy-turvy wind that couldn't make up its mind which way to blow. Lightning tore through the clouds, and thunder grumbled low in the distance. Big, far-apart drops of rain beat down on his face and chest. Wet as a beaver, he scrambled up the bank and yanked on his clothes, while Domingo offered deep rumblings of his own.

Peter thought, "If Dice had been here, he'd have barked and scolded us home at the first spit of rain." That would have spoiled all the fun. He leaped on Domingo's back while lightning forked cloud to cloud and earth-quaking thunder exploded.

Now Peter thought of nothing at all. He and Domingo loved the rush of wind with a wild and passionate love. There was nothing to stop them. They needled through the rain, sailing the dips and rises.

But of a sudden the whole world turned a ghastly green-

ish yellow. The wind hushed. Not a bird cheeped, nor a cricket. Peter felt fear pushing against his stomach, felt his heart beat noisy in his ears, and Domingo's heart thudding against his legs. They halted in the stillness, watching the thunderheads in the north spin into a crazy corkscrew. Clusters of little boiling black clouds bulged downward. And out of the tumbling mass came wisps of vapor like delicate garter snakes at play.

In but a few moments a big cloud dropped down into their midst. Peter had once seen a king snake spread its jaws for gorging. The big cloud was like that, now drawing into its mouth all the little ones. Victorious, the king now lashed his tail across the sky in a sinuous, twisting, skipping motion, and wherever it touched earth it sucked up strips of sod and spit them skyward in slivered fragments.

To Peter's dread, the lashing, hissing snake was coming straight at them. A tornado! They had to veer away, outrace the flying monster. Lightning leaped toward an approaching wagon train. In the vivid glare, Peter saw a blue bolt lace along the chain of four yoked oxen, saw it tail off in sulphurous fumes, leaving the four oxen standing, chained together, dead.

Domingo now became a fire-breathing dragon himself. Breath sucked out of lungs, legs pounding, he set the pace— swerving, spinning on his hocks, galloping seconds ahead of the roaring, rattling tail. Was the race hours long? Minutes? Or only seconds until the cloud-snake dissolved into nothing, and the sky laughed down at the earth and flung a rainbow over the wetness?

Peter could never tell how long Domingo had outrun the tornado. But as they jogged slowly for home, he knew unmistakably that the speed of San Domingo was as awesome as the forces of Nature.

Sodding Day

SUMMER WORE on, and every day the bond of union between Peter and Domingo tightened as together they explored the living, singing prairie.

Peter wished Time would stop still. Instead, autumn set in. Nights and mornings crackly cold. Days warm and hazy. Wildlife fully aware and winding up their own time clocks—bears lumbering off to caves, prairie dogs deepening their tunnels, beavers shoring up their dams, grackles ganging up in willow thickets, crickets clinging together in a solid ball. And Mrs. Lundy quietly reminding Mr. Lundy of the need for a new sod roof.

"Jethro?" she began one morning as she poured molasses over his pancakes. Hopefully she waited for recognition, but none came. The quiet was disturbed only by the coffee bubbling in its pot and the metallic ticking of the clock.

Peter waited, too. The silence made him jumpy, sent his mind flashing back to the letter in the treasure chest. Everywhere he looked—on the wall, on the blanket divider, on the checkered tablecloth—he saw his mother's handwriting:

... Jethro, as you know, has never been the same since that terrifying experience ... Someday, when Peter is old enough, I shall tell him the whole hideous story ...

Peter glanced sidelong at his father. He saw the fork poised an instant, thought some words might escape the bearded bunghole of a mouth. But none came. Instead, fork and knife went to work, severing the stack of pancakes into equal pie-piece quarters.

Peter looked down at his own plate—at the golden molasses oozing over his cakes. But he could not taste them until the silence broke.

Red in the face, his mother went on with the business of the morning. She ladled Aileen's oatmeal into her porringer. She poured the coffee from the heavy blue granite pot—Mr. Lundy's first, then Grandma's, and for Peter a half cup with cream added. Peter watched the cream eddy and swirl, but he could not drink.

The room remained silent, except for Grandma's spoon stirring and Mr. Lundy swishing the coffee in his mouth, cleaning his teeth.

Mrs. Lundy tried again. "Even Adam," she said, "noticed the sunflower growing out of our roof. And, Jethro, its roots are poking through, causing a sift of dust on my rag rug."

"So!" Mr. Lundy broke the silence with a grunt of mockery. "So Adam noticed that, too?"

"No, Jethro. Not that."

Meticulously, Mr. Lundy blotted up the last drop of molasses with the last morsel of pancake before he spoke again.

He pushed his plate aside and stood up, tall as God.

"I'll fetch you a dustpan," he said. "Got one only yesterday from an emigrant, along with all their cooking utensils."

"But what will his family do, Jethro, if they can't cook?"

Mr. Lundy's voice was matter-of-fact. "Their numbers dwindled, so they joined up with another train. Simple as that."

Grandma Lundy came out of one of her lapses. "Some of 'em sicken and die, eh?"

The toneless voice again: "We all got to die sometime. The weak and the scared first."

Mrs. Lundy shuddered, but her resolve suddenly strengthened. "We'll all sicken," she cried out, "unless you and Peter repair the roof before November rains chill us in our beds."

Grandma Lundy spoke up. "Big man! Big man!" she said, emphasizing the words with her spoon. "I abominate rain wettin' my blanket. It's bad enough if'n I do it my own self, but ain't no livin' excuse for a leaky roof."

Mr. Lundy snatched his hat from the wall peg just as a clump of straw from the ceiling fell onto his head and stuck in his hair. "What *I* abominate," he said, his voice icy, "is women's piddlin' prattle when I got a store to mind." Angrily he brushed the straw out of his hair, clamped his hat on his head, and banged out of the house, sending more straw falling.

Grandma cackled in delight. "Didn't that big man look funny with a straw tail hangin' onto his hair?" She hobbled over to her rocker and fell into it, shaking in laughter. "Tee-hee-hee . . . I wanted to thank Old Soddy for comin' to our rescue. 'Twas a right propishus moment, weren't it, for the sky to fall? Eh?" And she set to rocking wildly, laughing until the tears came.

Peter couldn't help joining in. But his laughter wasn't free

93

like Grandma's. She had no fear of the big man who once was her little boy.

Two nights later, the rain came slogging down on the soddy. From bedtime to dawn it gurgled between the grass-grown bricks, widening cracks into rifts.

In his sleep Peter dreamed Rawhide Creek was spilling over its banks and he and Domingo were caught in the current, trying to swim free, and an old cottonwood tree wrenched loose. And just when the tree came toppling on their heads, Grandma's wailing shook him awake.

"Help! Help! I'm a-drownding! Help me!"

For the rest of that night and all of the next, the family slept with papers over their heads and oilcloth over their blankets; and by day Grandma Lundy rocked underneath an open umbrella.

But before the week was out, the drip-drop from the roof stopped. Pots and pans were returned to their shelves, quilts and clothes aired to freshness, and the sky was a cloudless blue. No longer was there any excuse to put off repairing the roof.

One early morning Mr. Lundy stepped into Peter's path as the boy was on his way to the corral. "Come with me," he said abruptly.

Peter did not question. Two steps to one, he followed along to a draw-bottom where the buffalo grass grew thick and strong. Mr. Lundy plucked at his beard, pacing up and down, testing with his boots, appraising the spot. "It will do!" he said to the earth. Then to Peter: "Fetch me string."

Peter had to ask, "How much, Pa?"

"A hank of homespun. Your ma can wash it after."

For most of the morning Peter was more errand boy than

worker. He was glad to run here, there; to be able to talk to himself and to Dice if he felt like it. The only time his father spoke was to bark commands.

"Fetch me the spade."

"Fetch the ax."

"The grub hoe."

"Peel that small pile of saplings to make a skid."

"Hook Gabriel to the plow."

Curiously, it seemed to Peter that each time he began to hate his father, right afterward he found something in him to admire. Now it was the resolute, knowing way his father worked, the one-two-three absolute sureness of his movements. Here in the slough, his big boots were stepping off the remembered length of the roof; strong hands stringing out the wool for a guideline.

Even giddy Gabriel showed respect for Pa as together they turned over the furrows—each ribbon of earth the same width, each the same thickness. No frisking today. No balking. Today mule feet were pistons. Mule mind and mule muscle strained forward, answering human mind and muscle.

Yet more than he admired his father's skills, Peter stood in awe of his strength. Atlas, propping up the world with two bare arms, couldn't have been more muscle-powered than Pa. Who else could have rolled the huge strips of sod into bundles and heaved them single-handed onto the skid? And when the bundles were hauled to the house, any other man would have asked Peter to take the spade or ax and help chop them to size.

But Pa gloried in his strength—swinging the ax, chopping, swinging, chopping—slicing the sod into three-foot bricks. Peter was almost blinded by the sun glinting along the flashing blade.

Yet he could not take his eyes away. His mother must be watching, too, for in the doorway behind him he heard her singing in rhythm to the ax strokes. It *was* like music! And Ma singing to it:

"Ship ahoy! Ship ahoy! Ship ahoy!
We're whalers and sailors
And none of us tailors.
Ship ahoy! Ship ahoy! Ship ahoy!"

Sundown. And the new sod all in place, dirt side up, and Mr. Lundy and Peter working atop the new roof, filling the chinks with a plaster of mud. As they tamped it down, Peter felt a kind of harmony with his father. It was the first time they had ever worked side by side. Peter thought, "It must be like this to play in a band, sawing on a fiddle or blowing into a piccolo, the players each coming in at the right time to make the music swell." It was the same way now. His father sifting the dirt just when needed, and Peter tamping, tamping in time. In tune. Together. Even working around the chimney pipe they never lost a beat.

Pa had refused to come down at nooning and Peter had not wanted to either, even though he knew his mother would feel hurt. He'd make it up to her at suppertime. He'd lick his plate so clean she'd laugh and say, "Dice's tongue couldn't have done better." But now he had to hold on to this moment with his father, to make it last, and then maybe it would happen again—tomorrow, and all the tomorrows after.

It was Mr. Lundy who finally broke the rhythm. Straightening up, eyes shielded by the hand with the missing finger, he stood staring intently at a distant spot.

Peter turned to look. At first he saw nothing but a low smoke of dust curling slowly along the shadowy horizon. Then he too shielded his eyes, and now he imagined he could see a train of animals, like small paper cutouts against the big sky. But there was no white-topped settlers' wagon. Not a wagon of any kind—either up front or in the middle or trailing behind. There seemed to be no outrider or drover, either. Only this long parade of creatures spaced as orderly as the teeth in a rake.

Was it a mirage? Or were they real animals, traveling alone? Migrating? And what were they? Too small for humping buffalo! Too big for antelope! Making spyglasses of his fists, Peter sighted long ears nodding against the sky. "Of course," he thought, "they'd belong to mules." And he was sure he saw long legs forking; they had to belong to horses or mules. But one strange animal towered above the others; he was tall as some giant. Peter was puzzled.

Could this odd creature be a monster from long ago? Or a giraffe from Africa? He seemed to be leading the caravan. Yet with no human hand to guide him or his followers, how could they all be traveling in such an orderly procession?

Without comment Mr. Lundy returned to his work, dumping the last of the dirt on the last row of sod.

Peter tried to work, too, but the tail of his eye never left the cavalcade as it slowly wound down out of the sky and headed directly for Jethro Lundy's Trading Post & Smithy. As it drew closer, Peter could make out three dogs frisking along; or maybe, he figured, the smallest could be a cat. And there were large birds flapping, sometimes above the procession, or alighting on the backs of the bigger animals.

"Pe-*ter!*" Mr. Lundy's tone caught Peter unawares, nearly knocking him off the roof.

For minutes then Peter tamped with feet and hands both, not stealing so much as a glance, but listening with intense excitement to a man's voice, a rollicking, throbbing voice that carried across the prairie. The song came clear and clearer as the distance shortened:

> *"Oh, the Kings of Ireland*
> *They gave me birth,*
> *And I be royal too,*
> *Oh, I be royal too."*

Now big and little hoofbeats drumming. Why, they were heading not for the trading post but for the soddy! Peter could concentrate on his work no longer. He looked down and laughed at what he saw, and then he couldn't control his laughter. That tall creature he'd seen was three-in-one: a baby burro riding piggyback on a small man, who was sitting on a big mule! Oh, and the flapping birds he'd seen were banty hens and roosters! And there were cats—a tiger Tom and a calico; and a black dog and a white one; and horses and mules and a Jenny-burro and goats and a milk cow. They all seemed to be laughing with Peter—braying and cackling, barking and miaowing and mooing. Peter laughed so hard he rolled end over end and pitched headlong off the roof, at the man's feet!

Royal Son of Ireland

THE THUD of Peter's body brought a cry from the house. Mrs. Lundy came running, arms outstretched to help Peter. But Dice and the stranger were already at work—Dice licking the boy's face, the man opening Peter's shirt, listening to his heartbeat while all the animals looked on.

Up on the roof Mr. Lundy gave a final tamping here and there, making certain the work was completed to his satisfaction. Then he jumped down onto the wash bench by the door. From there he regarded Peter and pronounced judgment.

"Nothing wrong with him," he said, sure and confident. "Just winded, is all. The boy's chicken-livered." He stepped off the bench, slapping the dirt from his breeches, and completely ignoring the stranger, strode off to the trading post.

Peter lay gasping for breath. He felt as if a giant hand had thwacked him in the chest, shutting off his lungs. He tried to call after his father, to cry out, "Pa, wait! In just a minute I'll be better. Give me just a minute, Pa!" He *had* to explain.

"I can do my chores like always. I'm *not* chicken-livered, Pa!"

But it was no use. He couldn't utter a sound. He could only lie still, like a bird he'd watched die, its yellow beak agape. Would he die, too? The stranger seemed trying to breathe for him, gulping a great draught of air, crouching low over him. Suddenly the man's cheeks ballooned. His lips were touching Peter's. With steady force he pumped his own breath down Peter's gullet. Warm, moist breath, smelling strong of chewing tobacco. Peter coughed a thin, shallow cough. And then his gasps came closer and closer together. The man leaped back in triumph. The boy could suck his own air. He was breathing!

"Oh, merciful heavens be praised!" Mrs. Lundy drew in her own breath sharply. "And praise be to you, dear stranger."

"No more a stranger, ma'am. Name's Brislawn, or Breaslain, if'n you choose the Irish way to spell it." He took off his hat, made a kneeling bow, and with the brim rolled up in his hand, he turned and began fanning the boy's face.

"Either way," Mrs. Lundy said, "your name spells Friend for my son and me." Kneeling, too, she brushed the yellow hair, all damp with perspiration, from the boy's forehead.

"Ma!" Peter fought off tears. "I got to run after Pa. I got to explain I'm not chicken-liv . . ." He tried to sit up, but his hand grabbed his side in a spasm of pain.

"Ribs!" the little man exclaimed, as if he'd made a startling discovery. For an instant he looked toward his animals to check that none was missing, and saw each busy in its own way— grazing, nursing, picking and pecking, licking, or dozing. Satisfied, he squatted on the earth beside Peter. "Ah, here's the culprit," he said, spying a piece of petrified wood. "You must've landed on this."

He sat down carefully. "Now, son, you tell me when this hurts," he said, feeling the boy's ribs with slow, steady hands. Gradually the fingers worked toward the aching spot, testing, seeming to know what they would find. As they touched the two ribs over Peter's heart, the boy flinched.

Mr. Brislawn stopped at once. He fixed his eyes on Mrs. Lundy. " 'Pears to me," he said, looking professional yet sorrowful at the same time, " 'pears certain that his third and fourth ribs on the left side be cracked."

Mrs. Lundy's hand rose to her heart as if the pain were hers.

"There, there, little lady," Mr. Brislawn said. "You've a stout lad here. Nothing chicken-livered 'bout *him*. Besides," he said in a kind of quiet pride, "Friend Breaslain knows a thing or two about ribs—both man ribs and horse ribs. We'll talk more later as to that. But now," he said cheerily, "you run on into the house. Ready his bed and find me some wide elastic if'n you have it, or sheeting if'n you don't, and thread me a big needle."

"Yes, Doctor Brislawn. Oh, how lucky you came along just when you did."

"Sorry to disagree, ma'am, but likely the boy would never of fell off the roof if I hadn't of come along with my crazy caravan."

The little whiskery man neither denied nor accepted the title of doctor. "Now then," he said, "with yers and yer son's approval, I'll put my travelin' companions into yer corral. Then we'll see to the doctorin'. Son, you'll be all right meanwhiles?"

Peter managed a smile. Dice was lying beside him, and the doctor's coat over him. The pain had quieted, and the blood rushed warm all through him. He heard the doctor bunching his animals, calling each by name.

"Blacken! Penny! You round up Choctaw and Sweet Sioux. Nanny, quit buttin' me. Clarabelle, I'll be milkin' you soon and relievin' that big bag o' yourn. Tiger, stop clawing her. Jenny, yer little piggyback youngster looks all rested, don't he? That's a good mother ye are."

Above the tramping of feet and the snortings, brayings, and neighings, Peter heard Domingo's loud peal of greeting as the corral gate creaked open. He'd know that trumpety call anywhere . . . even in Timbuctoo, if there was such a place.

In the little while he was alone, Peter had time to think how a couple of broken ribs would shame him in the eyes of his father. He was sorry about that, for only a few moments ago they had been working together like a matched team. Now the rift between them would widen again. He wondered if this man Brislawn had a son, and if he'd like the boy less when hurt.

The man was singing in a grand tenor:

> *"Oh, the Kings of Ireland*
> *They gave me birth,*
> *And I be royal too,*
> *Oh, I be royal too."*

"I wish I had a father like . . ." Peter didn't finish the sentence, not even in his mind. God might punish him. Might smite his father dead. He did not like to think about death. He tried not to think at all as strong arms carried him into the house, set him on his bed, and skinned off his shirt.

"Let out all your breath, son. When I get through with you, ye're going to look like a horse wearing a cinch." Mr. Brislawn proceeded to wrap Peter round and round with strips of sheeting. "By the way," he asked, "I suppose you got another name aside 'son'?"

Peter laughed, then winced when it hurt. "Name's Peter," he sighed.

"And yer ma's name?" asked Mr. Brislawn, winding the

bandage tighter and reaching for the needle.

"She's Mrs. Lundy."

"And yer grandma?"

A shrill voice broke in. "Don't need no one to interduce me, young man. I'm Gran'ma Lundy."

"Pleased to meet you, ma'am. Yer callin' me 'young man' makes us best friends a'ready."

"And the baby?" he asked, sewing Peter's bandage securely in place.

Aileen toddled over to the stranger, putting up her hands to be lifted. "No baybee! No baybee! I'leen!"

"Well, I never . . .!" Mr. Brislawn took the child onto his knee and began dandling her to the tune of:

> *"This is the way the ladies ride,*
> *Prim, prim, prim.*
> *This is the way the gentlemen ride,*
> *Trim, trim, trim.*
> *And this is the way the farmers ride,*
> *A-hobbledehoy, a-hobbledehoy,*
> *And down ye go."*

Aileen squealed for more, while Mrs. Lundy, skillet in hand, sang along with the stranger until the little soddy was all laughter and song.

The gaiety ended abruptly as the door opened, letting in a gust of cold and Mr. Lundy. Wordlessly he hung his hat on the near buffalo horn, his coat and vest on the far one. In a single look he noted the extra place at table. His eyes demanded, "Why?" more plainly than if a dozen words had been spoken.

Mrs. Lundy answered. "Meet Doctor Brislawn, Jethro. He took care of Peter, bandaged his chest to ease the pain.

He's staying on a while."

Jethro Lundy's eyebrows climbed upward, almost into his thatch of hair. "A . . . while?" he repeated, stretching out the word until it chilled into years.

The man Brislawn gulped as though something were stuck in his throat. "Your boy," he said, "like to of killed himself. He landed on one of those rocks he'd been collecting."

No answer. No comment.

Peter opened his shirt to show the bandaging. Aileen hid behind her mother's skirts as quiet settled over the room.

Gently impatient, Mr. Brislawn filled in the silence. "The boy's got bruises, contusions, and fractures of the ribs."

"You a horse doctor or a people doctor?"

"Neither, sir."

The hush grew deeper, thicker, as Mr. Lundy glanced sidelong at the bandaging. "Neither, you say?"

Peter heard the rasp in his father's voice.

"Nope, neither! But I pride myself on a knack for doctorin', the way some folks got a green thumb for growin' things." His eyes twinkled and his rusty moustache went up, showing a row of small, tobacco-stained teeth. "Or," he added, "the way an uncommon man knows how to trade, benefitin' both himself and the pore soul on t'other side of the counter."

Mr. Lundy accepted the indirect compliment.

Peter sighed until his third and fourth ribs objected. But even with the pain he was relieved. There was no doubt about it. For a little while the man could stay.

Map of the Wild Lands

JETHRO LUNDY prided himself on two counts—his canniness at trading and his physical stamina. He never quite trusted anyone wholly, but when Mr. Brislawn touched on his ability to trade, the man became almost trustworthy in the eyes of Mr. Lundy.

Seldom had anyone stayed overnight with the Lundy household. Indians came to the door for handouts, and were sometimes invited to a sit-down-on-the-floor meal; and wayfarers occasionally joined the family at noon. But no one stayed on—not because the soddy was small and cramped, but because Jethro Lundy lived by rigid routine, with no time for joshing and chit-chat. He was king of his big world of the trading post and his small world of the soddy. Yet here was this whiskery stranger, with his goats and all, breaking into the pattern, threatening to dethrone him.

Mr. Brislawn, or Breaslain, communed mostly with animals. Nevertheless, he understood the nature of the human soul and mind as well, and was pleasantly unaware of his double gift. Having fathered three sons of his own, his heart went out to Peter, who had no brothers to fend for him, and a father who held him up to ridicule. It pained the man that he had been the cause of Peter's broken ribs. Aloud, to his horses, he said, "It'd be a good lick if I could help the boy step up a rung or two in the sight of his father. Is it," he asked of the pricked ears, "*intended* cruelty on the man's part, or does he gibe at the boy to ready him for life's harsher gibes? Or mebbe his bein' mean as a buzzard is a quirk he can't control—like a cowlick in the hair, or a nose too big for the face it prows?"

He longed to prove to the father that Peter was spunky for his size, manly for his age, and anything but chicken-livered. "I got to do it!" he told his animals. "Else those hurt and hungry eyes going to haunt me all my days."

After supper that evening, when the split-slab table was wiped clean and the oil lamp turned up, Mr. Lundy let his dark eyes slide to the stranger's. He would put the newcomer on the block for a bit of what? why? and where? It was a good way to poke holes in a stranger's story and send him flying on his way.

"Brisl'n!" He clipped the name short. "What brings you to this outpost of civilization?"

The little man let his mind ruminate back to the day when one of the top men in the United States Department of the Interior had tapped him on the shoulder, saying, "Bob, we hear you're able to draw contours or shoe a mule; you're *just* the man we need in the map department."

Jethro Lundy drummed the table, impatiently waiting his answer.

"The government!" Mr. Brislawn replied at last. It tickled him that he could be as chary of words as his examiner.

"Is that why you pack a surveyor's transit?"

"That's why."

Peter's eyes rounded in curiosity. His face asked, "What's a transit? How does it work?"

"In the morning," Mr. Brislawn said, "I'll show Peter how to look through the instrument. It took me a spell to know what to look for!" He chuckled in remembrance.

"It'll take *him* a longer spell," Jethro snorted.

"Mebbe so, but I doubt anyone could be slower'n me."

"No mebbe about it. The boy can read like a preacher. But by gobbs, when it comes to figures and things important, he blinks and blithers like a woman."

Mr. Brislawn looked at the boy, wanting to take the blows for him. To keep from snapping back at the father he busied his tongue, switching his cud of tobacco, cheek to cheek. He waited with tight lips for the next whipcrack of a question.

"How come you travel alone?"

"Fer safety."

"No Injun trouble?"

"Nope."

The answer irked Mr. Lundy. "How come *you're* immune when other folks tell of scalpings, poison arrows, and fires? You must be half crazy, man, travelin' alone."

"Ho, ho, ho! That's it!" Mr. Brislawn broke into a gust of laughter. "Injuns think me crazy—Sioux 'specially. They're like the Irish; they say, 'Crazy man already dead; can't kill dead man.' So they never try."

This satisfied Peter and his mother, who nodded in complete agreement. But Mr. Lundy resented the cockiness of his guest. He tried another tack. "No bear ever bother you?"

"Nope, nary a one." Mr. Brislawn twined his feet around the legs of his stool. He was enjoying the inquisition. "Y'see, a man's gotta be a teensy smarter'n bear."

Jethro bristled at some memory of his own. "How d'ye figure?"

"The way I do is look around sharp before making camp. If there's claw markings high on a tree, I figger *big* bear are about and I moves on to another campsite. Besides," he added, "I got po-lice protection."

"How so?"

"There's Blacken and Penny, my dogs, and Nanny and Billy-goat on guard, to say nothin' of Hee-hawin' Jenny. The ruckus they make'd send any bear hibernatin' outa season."

Mr. Lundy hadn't tripped the man yet. He made one more try. "If you're surveyin' for the government, what you doin' here, and where next?"

"Thought you'd never ask!" Mr. Brislawn frisked his whiskers in obvious pleasure. He fished into his vest pocket and came up with a piece of paper many times folded. Carefully he unfolded it and smoothed it out on the table. A strange excitement seized Peter. It was an important-looking paper, like none he had ever seen. Emblazoned at the top was a round blue seal, and below the seal a pen-and-ink map sprawled clear across the page.

A little gasp escaped Peter—not because his ribs hurt, but because he had never seen a handmade map, or any map, before.

The man's knuckly forefinger pointed. "Here's Missouri— St. Joseph, Missouri, known as the jumpin'-off place from the U.S. to the uncharted west."

"And you are charting it, eh, Brisl'n?" A tone of mockery crept into Mr. Lundy's voice.

Mr. Brislawn chose to disregard it.

" 'Zackly!" he said. "Us government men measure the shapes and areas, the highs and lows of the earth's surface."

"You *made* this map?" Peter asked, full of awe.

"Me and my transit, son. Now follow along. Right here, from St. Joe, me and my animals traipse along the big old Missouri River till it meets up with the Platte. Now we're here in Nebraska Territory where you've dug in; here where Injuns and buffalo are thicker'n measle spots."

Suddenly Aileen, bothered with colic or a dream, let out a shriek. Mr. Brislawn, without fuss or ado, moved his stool and map closer to the cradle, and with his foot rocking away and his small bright eyes remembering, he plunged into his trip. "First thing, I runs into a big party of Pawnees."

Creak-creak went Aileen's cradle as she quieted down, and creak-creak Grandma's rocker.

" 'Course the Pawnees was all mounted on tough, endurin' ponies which they had spirited away from the Comanches, and so I trade my big horses and got me the little Injun ponies you seen today. Then I join up with their party. About a hundred strong, we head west to Fort Kearney where, after a bit of tradin' and powwow, we part company, and I get busy surveyin' the lay o' the land."

The cradle and rocker never stopped. Nor did Mr. Brislawn.

"Speakin' o' tradin', Lundy, you'd have died of out-and-out pure admiration watchin' the Pawnees tradin' with the Comanches—blankets and beads, maize and moccasins for elegant Barb horses which the Comanches had stole from the Spanish grandees and missionaries. 'Course, in the dark o' night they'd often steal back their horses, and sometimes their blankets and corn!"

"What's a Barb horse, Brisl'n, and what makes him so all-fired special?"

"Fer one thing, his size."

"Size? I'd call yours peewee."

" 'Course you would! Which means he can stay tough and strong on less eats than a big critter. Second, he's low-crouped; keeps his back feet under him for good balance. And third, a Barb has got round leg bones 'stead of flat. He can head a cow or pull a plow, and can take poundin' travel day after day and won't pull up lame. He's what I call 'a get-there horse.' "

The clock bing-bonged the hour. One-two-three-four-five-six-seven-eight . . . Peter held his breath till the pain made him bite his lips. Who could go to bed now? But no one even mentioned bedtime. The Lundys were taking a trip with a little whiskery man, a big party of Indians, and enough animals to fill Noah's Ark.

"Where did you go from Fort Kearney, Doctor Brislawn?" Mrs. Lundy asked above the bonging.

"Waal, I met an old mountain man, and he said the Jesuit missionaries tried a shortcut to California back in 1776 and he'd tried it himself in 1835, and he recommended my going to California by way of Oregon. But I waved him good-bye quick as scat, and charted my own way along the river— writin' elevations here on my map for Ash Hollow, Chimney Rock, Scott's Bluff, till I come to Rawhide Creek—and here I be!"

A little silence fell over everyone as he folded the map back into its creases. Mr. Lundy stood up. "When you heading out, Brisl'n?"

"I was fixin' to move on in the morning, but"—he hesitated with a twist of a smile—"but my horses and mules, and Jenny, too, need well-fittin' shoes. And that little newborn burro has got to get better acquainted with his ma and a lot stronger afore I head for mountain country; I ain't goin' to make a habit of carryin' him piggyback."

Mrs. Lundy clapped her hands over her mouth, but her laughter came through anyway. "Did you ever?" she asked.

Peter could not keep quiet. "He did, Ma! That's why I fell off the roof. You should have seen him, Ma! Him riding the big mule and carrying the little burro on his back."

Mr. Lundy was figuring in his mind. "How many critters you say need shoein'?"

"Lemme see . . . there's my two Injun ponies I got from the Pawnees, and there's Sweet Sioux and Choctaw and Shoshone and the two mules, Ping and Pong, and Jenny Lind . . ."

"Hm . . . makes eight in all. Thirty-two shoes right there, *if* they wear front *and* hind. Eh, Brisl'n?"

"Front and back both get shod. I don't like my critters' feet to spread out like a duck's. Guess I'm the onliest man in the West who shoes his mules."

Mr. Lundy ended the conversation. "Our alarm clock bells at four," he said. "We'll get the shoeing done early so's you can be on your way, case you change your mind." Then he stepped outdoors, clearing his throat like a bellowing bull.

Mr. Brislawn shook his head at the thought of anyone needing an artificial wake-up. "I sleep outdoors," he said. "Even rooms airy as this one bind me in, make me feel all constricted, like I was a cob o' corn trapped in a husk." He got up, smiling at Peter and running his fingers up the back of his head.

"As fer wakin' up, there ain't no more dependable alarum than my banty rooster and Jenny Lind singin' a duet. Good night, my friends."

"If a Hand Be Four Inches..."

THE RUGGED little man with the intense blue eyes stayed on. And an aura of such contentment filled the soddy that everyday-living took on a kind of glory. He belonged suddenly to each person.

To Peter he was doctor and counselor.

To Aileen he was "Bris-lee-ee!" Always to be counted on for a gay, hobbledehoy ride.

To Grandma he was a familiar spirit out of her past— a leprechaun from her childhood, bringing her surprises each day: a tiny stone of glittering crystal, a sunshine-yellow aspen leaf, or the last of the wild plums.

To Peter's mother he was someone to sing with, to laugh and cry with. He twisted slough hay for her fire; helped her wind yarn and make Irish stew rich in onions; he admired her album of pictures. And whenever Mr. Lundy belittled Peter, he sent her a look of such compassion that she was able to bear the shared hurt.

As for Mr. Lundy, he felt smug in the shrewdness of his bargain. In exchange for three meals a day, the mapmaker was doing Peter's chores, including the graining and watering of livestock, and the early morning doctoring as well. He knew all manner of doctor tricks: how to make boots of water-soaked buffalo hide, nailing them to the hooves of footsore horses so that the hide shrank around their bruised feet like protective socks. Alum mixed with goose grease was his remedy for saddle or harness sores; sal soda his prescription for infection from bites. There seemed no end to his store of knowledge, nor to the supplies in his packs. Besides, Mr. Lundy now felt free to go off hunting for a day or two, knowing a steady man was in charge, someone who could talk Indian or horse, and doctor man or beast if need be.

When Mr. Lundy was away, evenings were spent in merrymaking. Out came a zither-box with its world of strings, and music sprouted like grass after rain. Fingers plucking, feet tapping, Brislawn's rich tenor swirled and swelled until the wind in the stovepipe whistled in concert. Marches, lullabies, dirges, opera, folk tunes—Brislawn's fingers played them all, while his heart and voice sang the words. "Angels with their golden harps," Peter thought, "could make no finer music." The moment the man touched on a familiar tune, the family chimed in lustily:

> *"We cross the prairie—as of old*
> *Our fathers crossed the sea—*
> *To make the West as they the East*
> *The homestead of the free."*

Grandma's reedy voice quavered and strung out the "free-ee-ee." " 'Tis my favoritest of all," she sighed.

Sometimes the songs were in Gaelic, sad and haunting. Peter made his lips move as if he knew the words, and his silent singing felt strong within him. Whenever Mrs. Lundy was moved to tears, Brislawn quickly changed to doggerel:

"Music hath charms to quell a savage,
Rend an oak, or split a cabbage."

For Peter, the autumn of his broken ribs was a time of healing—body and soul. Brislawn made him feel important. When they talked, the man listened intently, cocking his head, making certain he heard every word. Then in his fatherliness he would answer man-to-man. Equal.

It was a time of learning, too, without any pain or embarrassment. One day it would be the mystery of arithmetic. Numbers were fun when the problems had something to do with horses and history.

"Peter, your San Domingo measures thirteen and a half hands high."

"He does?" Peter asked, wondering if this were good or bad. It was midmorning, after chores, and they were sitting at the kitchen table, mending goose-quill pens.

"Yup, and a fair size that is—for an Injun pony."

Peter smiled with relief.

"My little burro, Jackie," Brislawn went on, "is only seven hands high. Now what I'd be pleasured to know, is the difference between the two. In inches."

Peter took up a freshly mended pen, puzzling where or how to begin. There was a little silence.

"Oh, it clean skipped my mind to tell you that a hand equals four inches. You see," Mr. Brislawn explained, "long years ago in England, and 'specially Ireland, folks spoke of their ponies and hunters as bein' so many hands high."

Peter was unafraid to ask, "But, Brisley,"—the affection-ate nickname slipped out unnoticed—"what if some hands are big like Adam's and Pa's? And some smaller, like yours and Ma's?"

"In their wisdom, son, the Irish just took an average and come up with four inches."

Peter studied his own hand. "Why, mine measures more'n that!"

Mr. Brislawn laughed heartily. "Here's what I calls a thinkin' lad," he said, turning to Mrs. Lundy. "He's countin' wrist to fingertips, whereas our ancestors held the hand hori-zontal but measured vertical—across the palm. Like this." He juxtaposed his hands, one atop the other, to illustrate. "And that's the way 'tis to this day."

Grandma and Aileen, in their close-related worlds, copied the action hand-on-hand. It would be a new game for them to play, long after their beloved friend had gone.

"Now, then, Peter, figger aloud if you've a mind to, and take all the time needed. I ain't due in California today, y'know." He got up from the table and went over to Grandma, inviting himself to string beads with her.

Grandma squeaked in ecstasy. "Emily!" she called. "Fix tea for my company. Tea with milk and honey, Emily!"

Only too willing to stop her weaving, Mrs. Lundy put the kettle on. It was near nooning time anyway and she would make enough for all. How pleasant it was to hear Peter mumbling happily as he figured. "If a hand be four inches, then thirteen hands'd be four times thirteen. Lemme see . . . four times three is twelve, one to carry. Four times one is four, and plus one'd be fifty-two inches. And then a half hand'd make two more inches." Under his breath he whispered triumphantly, "I've got the answer! It's fifty-four inches!"

Purposely Mr. Brislawn dropped one of the beads so it rolled toward Peter's stool. He reached out for it, smiling. "Fifty-four inches is 'zactly right. Why, it didn't take you no more'n a whisker of time. Now, what's yer next step?"

Peter felt a mounting sense of excitement. His mind was sharp and ready. Jackie's height would be easy to figure. "Four inches times seven'd be twenty-eight, and twenty-eight from fifty-four leaves twenty-six. Quick as scat he handed his answer to Brislawn:

The difference in height between San Domingo and Jackie is 26 inches, or 6½ hands.

If someone had given the little man a bag of gold, he couldn't have acted more tickled. His blue eyes shone and he broke into a rollicking laugh.

Mr. Lundy's hand on the latch didn't stop his laughter or his saying to Peter, "I don't want to make any brags, but either I'm a better teacher than I used to be, or you're a sight smarter'n any other boy yer age, and that includes me own."

Without changing expression, Mr. Lundy heard but made no comment. Inwardly his smugness grew. In addition to a doctor, he'd hired a schoolteacher. Without pay!

Pure Spanish Barb

PETER THREW himself into learning, hoping to keep his teacher from gazing far off, like a horse dreaming of hightailing it to the hills.

And he stretched out his invalid days as long as he could. But as his ribs healed, he began, without thinking, to lift, to carry, to chop. In the midst of a chore, he would suddenly remember, and let his ax fall or his load drop as if stabbed by a spasm of pain. Instantly the little man would rush in to finish the job, murmuring, "Here, here, son. Let me do this whilst you set down and give yer ribs a chance to heal."

Peter was ashamed, then. But how else could he hold onto these days of companionship?

One morning he completely forgot his playacting. He ran from well to house carrying two heavy buckets of water on his neck yoke. When he came out again, his beloved friend was sitting on the wash bench whistling merrily as he cleaned his gun. He seemed totally unaware of the rest of the world.

For a long while Peter stood by, watching. With the gun cleaned, the man took off his boots and put on a pair of moccasins. He whisked the dust from his boots and oiled them carefully, as though he were about to set out on a journey. Peter felt a sense of loneliness, as though the man were already disappearing into distance. If only the old well had been dry! If only he'd fallen in and maybe broken another rib! How could Brislawn think of leaving? Taking all his happiness along? And likely singing as he went:

> *"Oh, the Kings of Ireland*
> *They gave me birth . . ."*

Miserable, Peter turned and went into the house. He sat down in his place at the table, facing the window, watching. He saw Brislawn put on his boots and walk spry-legged across the road to the corral.

"Hungry?" his mother asked.

"No, Ma."

His mother was putting something into a small sack and tying it securely: "Journey cake, probably," Peter told himself.

"He's fixin' to go, ain't he, Ma?"

Without waiting for an answer, Peter suddenly dashed out of the house, cut across the road, and leaped the corral fence.

Mr. Brislawn, looking every inch the surveyor and mapmaker for the United States government, was saddling up.

"Brisley!" Peter wrenched out the name. "You can't be leavin' without sayin' so?"

"Who, me? Leavin'?" With the cinch buckled, the man looked across the horse's withers. "No, 'course not! Leastwise, not till tomorrow." He broke out in laughter. "Today's *today*."

"But where you going?"

"Y'mean, where *we* goin'. Any invalid that can heist a keg
of nails one day and shoulder two pails o' water the next can

speed the parting guest with a farewell powwow. Look! Here comes our vittles."

Peter swung around. His mother was hurrying toward them, waving the brown sack he had seen her tying.

"You knew?" Peter asked her as she handed the bulging package to Brislawn.

"Ever since yesterday we've been planning. Our good friend *is* leaving tomorrow, but today is for skylarking. Your father knows," she added.

"Did he say yes?"

With firm assurance Mrs. Lundy smiled. "He didn't say no."

. . .

Off into the ocean of grass the three dogs—Dice, Blacken, and Penny—led the way, tails waving in a frenzy of bliss.

It was a day of sun and sparkle. A skim of snow had fallen the night before, washing sage and buffalo grass. It seemed as if the world had been swept clean for their holiday. The sun warmed their backs, the wind blew for their pleasure. They sucked it deep into their lungs. Swinging along bareback on Domingo, following the little man on Choctaw, seemed as wondrous to Peter as riding tandem with the Lord beside the still waters of Rawhide Creek.

Peter trotted up and glanced sidelong at Brislawn. "Why, he's almost all hat!" he noted in alarm. "A big wind could blow him clean through a house, like he was a straw." Under the brim of his hat the man's eyes were busy, scanning the buttes far distant and the game trails close by.

Watching him, Peter reasoned, "Three weeks ago he saved my life. Now it's my turn to help him." His mind went skipping for ideas; suddenly his voice clamored for attention.

"Brisley . . . sir . . . could we, I mean Domingo and me . . . could we ride out with you tomorrow?"

The man was singing lustily:

> *"Oh, I was born in Ireland*
> *One night when I was young . . ."*

The rest of the words turned into humming as if to ready an answer.

Peter tried again, more urgently. "Sir! I could set up your tripod and plane table; I could be your recorder. And a prospector taught me how to throw a diamond hitch; I could pack all your gear. And I could make camp and cook rice without its boiling over. And I could . . ."

The humming stopped. Penny, Blacken, and Dice had struck rabbit scent and were yapping in pursuit.

Brislawn twisted half around in his saddle. "Hound music is prettier'n man's any day, ain't it?" Then looking straight at Peter he said, "I'm honorated by yer wanting to come. If we both was five year older, or even two, I'd snap up yer offer quick as an eye wink."

"But I *feel* old, Brisley. And you yourself told Pa I was quicker'n any other boy my own age. And I'm strong!"

"Yes, yes, I know. And besides bein' old for yer years and quick, ye're spunky as a dog with his first porcupine. 'Tain't that at all, at all. It's yer ma."

"*My ma?*"

"Yup. She needs you until little Aileen can be the comfort you are."

Mr. Brislawn pulled up to a halt. "There'll be a right time to go, son," he said. "And you'll know for certain when that time comes."

"How'll I know?"

A band of wild horses crowned a slope in the distance. Bugles and whinnies cross-fired over the plain.

Mr. Brislawn paused, wanting to be sure Peter was listening. "Ever hear of a writin' man, name of Cervantes?"

"No, sir."

"Wa-al, my grandsire of County Donegal—he's the one spelled his name O'Breaslain—he used to read to me from a book called *Don Quixote* which was writ by this feller Cervantes. I can recomember the best part, word for word."

"What *was* the best part?" Peter asked as the wild horses disappeared. "And why isn't your name O'Breaslain anymore?"

Mr. Brislawn chuckled. "As to yer last question, only way I can figger is my gran'ther dropped the 'O' in the ocean coming over."

"Maybe he wanted to be American in a hurry," Peter suggested.

"Could be just that. Now as to *Don Quixote* . . ." The little man's voice changed to a high quavering, as if he were his own grandfather. " 'There's a time for some things,' " he intoned, " 'and there's a time for all things; a time for great things, and a time for small things.' "

"But how will I know when it's the time for great things?"

"I'm a mystic, son, like all the Irish, and I prophesy you'll know for dead certain when the time comes."

The two horses were pawing, growing restive, inching toward each other. Choctaw touched nostrils with Domingo, who let out a squeal in pretended fierceness. Then he sneezed in Choctaw's face.

Brislawn exploded with laughter. "They're bored with our

palaver, and spoilin' for action." He pointed to a golden eagle cleaving the sky. "Let's fly!"

With barely a touch the two mustangs struck off in unison, bolting through the rustly grass at a full gallop, catching up to the hounds still on the line of rabbit. The eagle soared over them, a winged pacesetter. Neither horse minded uneven ground, but went faster and faster and would not be headed. Domingo, enjoying himself, trumpeted to the heavens, frightening everything in his way. A pronghorn buck sent his harem of does dashing for safety in bounding leaps. A sage hen squawked skyward.

Peter felt Domingo's body springy beneath him, felt him turn on his speed to pass Choctaw. What did he know of politeness to a royal Irishman from County Donegal?

Choctaw's ears laced back. He lengthened his stride, galloping beat for beat with Domingo, up a swell of hill, over and down, up the next and down, up and over and down until at last Domingo sailed ahead and Brislawn pulled up, laughing, calling to Peter to swing his horse around.

"Ho, ho, ho!" he cried. "I knew it! I knew it!"

Peter turned back to join him. He was laughing, too, in sheer animal joy. He caught Brislawn's excitement. "Knew what? Knew what?"

"Oh, yes, yes, yes. I knew it! I knew it! Pure Spanish Barb! Pure Andaluz!"

Peter hated to interrupt, to spoil the man's triumph of knowing whatever it was he knew.

"Son!" Mr. Brislawn cried. "Do you know what horse-god you're riding?"

"Is it Spanish? Is it Anda . . .?"

"Yes, yes, yes. Andaluz. But more!" The words quickened.

"When the Sioux let you keep Domingo, they knew the prize they were giving, but do you?"

Peter laughed breathlessly. "Yes, yes, yes!" he exclaimed, copying Brislawn. "A faster horse there never was!"

"But more, Peter! More!" He put Choctaw into a dogtrot. "That colored bonnet over his ears! He's a Medicine Hat!"

"He is?"

"He is, he is! To Injuns he's Big Medicine. Sacred. A god. Nothing can harm his rider. Not slingstone nor arrow. Not rifle ball nor lightnin'."

Peter grinned. "That ought to please Ma!"

"And his ribs!"

"What about his ribs?"

Brislawn was chuckling with his secret knowledge. His eyes shone. "This, now, is something revolutionary. Only a few of us knows. Y'see, little Barb horses has but seventeen pairs o' ribs, or less. That's proof o' their authentication. Big man-made horses, howsomever, has eighteen pairs!" He gave Choctaw a joyful smack on the rump. "I calls the big ones man-tinkered horses, while Choctaw and Domingo—they're *puro Español.* They can outlast the big ones any day.

"And another thing . . ." He slowed Choctaw to a walk and his words came out slowly, thoughtfully. "And another thing," he repeated, "their spinal colyums is one more proof of purity. Our Spanish Barbs has five lumbar vertebrae whilst the man-made tinkered horses has six."

"But, sir, how can you tell till they're dead?"

"Oh, there be other signs, too."

"Like what?"

"Our horses has crescent-shaped nostrils and short backs, and the legs in front make an upside-down V, like both legs is growin' outa the same hole. They're not like some of the tinkered horses with a leg square on each corner, like a table.

"I 'spected you'd like to see how 'tis, so last night I diagrammed you some pictures of the diff'rences between our purebloods and the man-made horse. You jes' keep these for ref'rence." And he handed over the sketches.

Peter studied them as he rode, while Brislawn talked on like a wound-up toy. "Away west o' here, I got me a homestead nestled in the Red Fox Hills a mile back from the Oregon Trail. That's where the Spanish Barb ponies and the red foxes run strong. Yup," he added wistfully, "I got me a little shack there for my old days, and a root cellar that's never seed a carrot or turnip."

"Bones in it?" Peter asked, grinning.

"Yep, ribs and vertebrae of the loyal mustangs who've taken the long, long trail. Someday you'll come there to see the proof o' purity, and me."

He slid down from his horse and examined Domingo carefully. "Hmmm, round-boned from knees and hocks down. Forelegs straight as a rule. Chest deep. And legs V'd up nice. Why, this feller could go thirty mile and back the same day! He could walk flat-footed fifty mile in less'n ten hours!"

Suddenly Mr. Brislawn let out a whistle. "Well, I'll be hog-tied! I jest noticed your Barb is minus any chestnuts on the insides of his legs! Now you'll allus be able to identify him!"

"I could anyhow."

"Mebbe yes, mebbe no. Horse thieves're mighty clever at paint-daubin' and disguisin' even a Medicine Hat."

Peter grew light-headed with excitement. He had always known Domingo was special, but to have a horseman like Brislawn say so made it gospel true.

They stopped at noon beside an Indian moon calendar with rays of stones laid out on the earth like spokes of a wheel, the hub a buffalo skull. In friendly silence they ate their lunch, sharing corn bread and jerky with their dogs, and apples with their horses.

On the quiet way home Brislawn suddenly said, "For my little Choctaw stallion that I caught in the Stairstep Mountains, and my mare Sweet Sioux, how would you like to trade Domingo?"

The words spurted out like air from the bellows. "What kind of trading was this?" Peter thought. "God-high praise for Domingo, and then the offer! Most men scoff at the horse they want, call him a mangy rat or worse, figuring to buy him cheap."

Peter tried to let his mind play with the idea, the way Pa would. Sweet Sioux and Choctaw together could have many colts. Enough so he could have a band of his own, and they could travel to Laramie Peak and on to far places. In a leap of imagination he saw each colt and filly. He laughed outright. Not any of them, nor all of them together, could equal one San Domingo.

Brislawn took the silence for indecision. "How 'bout if'n I throw in Billy-goat and Nanny?"

Peter let out his breath in a long sigh. "Thank you, Brisley, sir, but y'see, Domingo and me are teamed up for life. He's not for trading. *Ever.*"

Stranger on Horseback

IN THE middle of the night, with a full moon for his lantern, Robert O'Breaslain from County Donegal finished loading his mules, Ping and Pong; his stallion, Choctaw; and the burro, Jenny Lind. Everything, from delicate instruments to shovel and frying pan, was stowed in its precise place. Then he saddled up Sweet Sioux, tied his bedroll to the saddle, levered himself up, and was about to ride out when the door of the soddy flew open.

Gabriel, braying his good-bye to Jenny Lind, had awakened the entire family. Peter and his father arrived at the corral almost at the same moment. Unable to hide his pleasure over the departure, Mr. Lundy was no longer miserly with his words.

"G'morning, Brisl'n," he said affably. "A strong east wind's a-blowing; you should make twenty-thirty mile today, easy. I see you're all rigged up and rarin' to go."

"Yup. Time to eat my dust as a rover must."

The little man looked straight at Jethro Lundy, but the

words were marked for Peter. "I prize the time I had here," he said, "and I thank ye for your home and fireside."

Peter's father made a stab at returning the politeness. "And I'm obliged to ye for teachin' the boy to add, s'tract, and divide."

" 'Twas easy, Lundy. The boy's smarter'n a treeful of owls. But you learned him something I couldn't."

"How's that?"

"I tell you, Lundy, yer old hatband would of split in two if'n you'd heard him turn down my tradin' offer!"

From behind them came a caterwauling of commotion— the goats butting each other; cats hissing and berating Dice; the rooster crowing to the dawn; Ping, Pong, and Jenny answering Gabriel with raucous brays.

Peter felt a prickle of alarm. He watched his father's face tighten, heard him out-bellow the animals to silence. Then the penetrating voice snapped: "Your offer, Brisl'n? What was it?"

"Why, 'twas two of my pure-blooded Spanish Barb mustangs in trade for little Domingo. Y'see, Lundy, the lad was dead right to turn me down."

"How so?"

"Without knowing, he felt that his stallion was sacred. Only a boy that Injuns loved would be allowed to keep a pure Medicine Hat. Lundy, you yerself know that most horses on the trail give out; you've got a corral full of 'em. But Domingo is ready any day for a fifty-mile ride!"

Jethro Lundy's eyes narrowed; the iris and pupil seemed to disappear until only slits of white showed. When he opened them again, his face was inscrutable. He started to speak, but the noise of the animals changed his mind. He strode off to the trading post without a good-bye.

Brislawn slipped down from Sweet Sioux and went over to Peter. He put his hand lightly on the boy's shoulder. "Once," he said, "my brother Ferdie and me got into a wild stampede for gold in the Black Mountains."

Reaching into his pocket, he took out a piece of bone looking very white in the dawn, except for one end which shone with a gold capping. He pressed the trinket into Peter's hand.

Peter felt of its warm shininess.

"It's an elk's tooth I found there in the foothills," Brislawn explained with a chuckle. "I panned barely enough gold to fill it. You keep it as a wee meemento of the fun days we had. It'll allus be worth a dollar; mebbe two."

Peter managed to nod his thanks.

"Now, son, don't watch me out of sight; that's a strict Irish taboo."

Peter spoke his first words of the morning. "What would happen, Brisley, if I did?"

"We'd never set eyes on each other again in this world."

"Then I won't watch," Peter said, swallowing his sorrow. The soddy door opened, and he heard Aileen crying out, "Brislee-eee!" and his mother calling, "God be with you."

He saw the little man climb aboard his mare, lift his hat in salute, and ride out. When all his caravan had fallen into place, following him, Peter closed the gate and turned his back, covering his face. Leaning against the fence, he listened until his ears hurt. Brislawn hadn't said he could not listen. He waited a long time, waited for the ringing, rollicking words,

"Oh, the Kings of Ireland . . ."

But there was no song. None at all. Only the drumming hoofbeats dying away into nothing.

134

With Mr. Brislawn gone, a stillness fell over the soddy, and didn't lift with the days. Everyone seemed changed. Mrs. Lundy sang less, and laughed hardly ever. Aileen became cross and peevish. Grandma slumped in her chair by day and babbled in her sleep by night: "Oh, the Kings of Ireland, they gave me birth . . . Oh, the Kings . . ."

Peter hid his feelings in silence. Always before, Mr. Lundy had been given to long, moody silences. Now Peter held his tongue, while his father stormed and howled and called Brislawn "that disputatious, interferin' Irish disrupter of homes."

One day when the father could bear the boy's stillness no longer, he sent him off on the early stage to Fort Laramie, twelve miles away. His errand was to deposit some orders at the post office there, and to bring back two heavy steel drills and a tool for removing wagon tire bolts. Peter wondered whether this was the time to run away; he'd think about it during the trip. But without Domingo, what fun would there be? And how would he travel?

With the mail and eight silver dollars in his pocket he boarded the stage, curiously noting a horseman who stayed behind at the trading post. He was not bullwhacker nor herder nor outrider. He looked like an important man from the United States, and he sat a tall, rangy Thoroughbred that Brislawn would have called a man-tinkered horse. Peter thought about Brislawn as he wedged in between his fellow passengers, figuring where he might be by now, and wondering if the little burro slowed him down any.

Then the stage started, and he forgot everyone and everything in the pitching and tossing of the coach as it went jouncing over the plain.

• • •

Fort Laramie was trading post, blockhouses, soldiers' barracks, storehouse, and post office. The bigness and bustle of the place bewildered Peter and hurt his ears. He did his errands at once and was glad to catch an eastbound stage for home. The driver, a jolly fellow, invited him to sit up on the box beside him and regaled him with the peculiarities of his team of six mules—the ticklish ears of Tom, the handy heels of Harry, the rearin' Wheeler—until Peter knew them all, plus some thunderous new cuss words.

With his bullhide whip and his talk, the driver made time and distance fly, so that Peter was back at his own trading post to water and feed Domingo himself with daylight to spare. Dice met him with a brief wagging of his tail, then a whine. He took a few steps toward the corral, stopping to see if Peter followed.

"Wait, boy! Just let me deliver the tools first."

The trading post was humming, as usual. Peter laid the tools on Adam's bench and ran out before his name was called.

"I'll beat you to the corral," he told Dice. And the two broke into a wild dash.

Halfway there Peter saw new heads lifting. He ran faster, squinting to make out a big horse, new oxen, and a span of mules. Then his eyes strained for Domingo. He whistled for him, but only Gabriel answered. With Dice nosing ahead, he ran searching in and out of the sheds that lined one side of the corral. All the other animals, new and old, followed out of curiosity.

In the pit of his stomach Peter felt the beginnings of terror. He cried to Dice, "Find Domingo!" Together they ran along the corral fence, Dice snuffing audibly beneath, Peter scanning the rails. None was missing. None even broken.

Peter ran back across the rutty road, stumbling and picking himself up again, the sickness in his stomach worsening. Inside the shop he darted around people, casks, and kegs, firing questions at his father: "Where *is* Domingo? What's happened to him? And oh, Pa, why?"

Jethro Lundy's eyes were cold as glass. "I've customers," he said. He shut the boy out of his consciousness. It was as though a door had slammed in Peter's face, and the force of its slamming chilled him.

Outside, a cold, clean wind blew from the north. A glimmer of yellow light shone in the soddy, but Peter turned from it. Step by slow step, he and Dice went around to the back of the shop and hid behind a clump of sage. In the gathering dark he heard wagons pull away, heard his father clump down the two wooden steps and head for home and supper.

With heart growing heavier, Peter waited until he heard Adam whistling, rattling his frying pan and coffeepot. Then he went around to the big front door. It was closed, the latchstring pulled in. "Adam!" Peter called. And all in a moment he was caught up in the giant arms.

"He knows," Peter thought; "he knows and he cares."

"Put me down, Adam! I've got to know. Is he dead? Is he . . . sold?"

Buffalo steak frying over the heat of the forge needed turning. Adam used the hoof parer for the job. He motioned Peter to sit down on an upturned keg.

"I can't, Adam. Talk to me. Tell me!"

There was no sound in the shop, except for the meat sputtering in the fat, and Dice snuffling with upraised nose. Adam turned around, his face contorted with suffering. He ran his hands over his bald head as if he were pulling chunks of hair out by the roots. "Gawblimy, blimy," he mumbled in despair.

Peter stood rigid and quiet, feeling sorrow for Adam, for his having to tell whatever it was he had to tell.

At last the words came of themselves: "Come to think on it, Little Brother," Adam said, "you missed him by the eensiest hair."

"Missed who?"

"The man."

"What man, Adam?"

"The man on the big horse."

"Where was he going? Where does he live? Did you hear his name? Who was he, Adam?"

"He weren't wicked, Peter. He give me some good eatin' tobacco." Adam spat as if to prove his point.

"But *who was* he?"

A light came to Adam's eyes. "His name were Al-ex-an-der Majors! And his horse were bald, like me. Bald Gallow-way 'twas his horse's name." He grinned, happy and relieved at remembering. Now there was no stopping him. "Little Brother, him owns six thousand wagon trains and a mee-millionth of oxen to pull 'em. Twelve to ever' wagon. And he freights clean to . . ."

"Then why did he need Domingo?"

"Him wanted a dandy little Indian pony for his three girls."

"But why did it have to be Domingo?"

Adam rubbed his head fiercely. "Mebbe he's addled from riches. Has to have whate'er he see."

"But Pa? How could Pa . . .?"

"Yer pa says, 'No, the pony belongs to son, Peter.' And he says 'No' and 'No' till the man kept on. First 'twas only two ox."

"And then?"

"Two more, and another two. And a span o' mules."

"And then?"

"His own big horse, Bald Gallow-way . . . coming five next grass. 'Twas then yer Pa says . . ."

"Says what, Adam? What'd he say?"

" 'That big horse should please the boy,' he says. I remember jes' as plain."

The steak charred, and only Dice found it to his liking. The coffee boiled over. Peter stayed that night in the loft, with Adam giving up his own bunk, buffalo robe and all. Once Adam tiptoed down the ladder and disappeared to tell Mrs. Lundy her boy was safe. Back in the loft, he put on his nightcap and rolled up in a blanket on the floor, a giant mummy.

Peter lay awake, staring numbly into darkness, unable to cry. Toward morning he fell into a thrashing sleep. Adam, calling out in a dream, brought him sharp awake: "Don't do it, Mr. Lundy! Don't do it; the boy'll never fergive ye. Oh, Gawblimy, Gawblimy."

It was Adam's crying that wrenched the silence.

The Withered Hand

EVEN AS Peter examined Bald Galloway next morning his mind was made up. He would put on his other shirt under the one he was wearing, and his other socks on top of those he had on, and no one would have any notion he was going away. As he headed toward home he saw his old wheelbarrow leaning against the soddy, and he thought of a time long ago when he was five, and he had tried to push it with a load of buffalo chips but he couldn't budge the stubborn thing. And his father had laughed, calling him a puny tomtit. He remembered how he had burst into tears, and then he remembered his mother running with him into the house and holding him on her lap, close by the fire, and he could feel her strength moving into him.

But that was long ago, and now he was fourteen and he put up a barrier against pity.

Emily Lundy understood. From her window she watched him scuffing the dirt as he walked, not glancing back at his

big new horse, nor paying attention to Dice's invitation to play. When he stopped dead still and leaned against the saplings that closed in the corral, she threw on her shawl and went out to him. A cool mist hung over the morning, making the world seem masked and unreal.

Without looking, Peter knew that his mother had come out to comfort him. He wished she hadn't. If she could tolerate his father, then . . . He never finished the thought. Perhaps the man was not even his father, him so dark-eyed and dark-haired.

A silence closed around them, and the silence had a life of its own that even the clacking of wild geese could not penetrate. Time itself stood still and waiting.

After a while Peter said, "You'll get cold, Ma, with only that little shawl. You better go back."

"I can stay only a moment, Peter, but what I have to tell you may make you strong enough to stand up under the weight of your sorrow."

"Not anything could," Peter thought. Nothing she said could matter or put his world back together again.

"Let me tell the story quickly, son, without stopping, for fear I might not go on."

The clacking of the geese came louder, then slowly died away.

"Your father," the troubled voice began.

Peter winced. Did it have to begin with him?

Mrs. Lundy tried again. "What happened to make your father bitter is no fault of his."

"Whose is it?" Peter demanded.

"I explain for him," her quiet voice went on, "because he will not defend himself. While you were still a child, he lived through an agony that would have killed a lesser man."

Suddenly Peter was again sick with the quinsy, and he was opening a letter not meant for him, and the words quickened in his mind:

> . . . *Jethro, as you know, has never been the same since that terrifying experience.*

"Your father," Mrs. Lundy continued, her voice impassive, "used to guide men over the mountains. Some were gold seekers, some missionaries, and some were nesters who feared Indians and road agents. Often he would ride on ahead, hunting bear, elk, deer, or wild turkey—whatever he could find—and by the time the party caught up he'd have a fire going and meat simmering in the pot.

"One day," her voice fell to a whisper, "when your father was alone on the trail, his horse pulled up lame and he dismounted to set a loose shoe. Out of nowhere a grizzly she-bear pounced on him, clawing and biting, until the flesh of his legs was in shreds. One arm, too, was mangled; that's how he lost his finger. When the party caught up, your father was close to death." Mrs. Lundy stopped for breath. Peter said nothing. His eyes were fixed on the mist rising.

"With your father's directions," she went on, "the men decided to go on anyway, taking his horse as a spare. But in all fairness they did leave one of the gold seekers behind to stay with him the few hours he had left, and to give him a decent burial in his own blanket.

"But Jethro Lundy willed himself to live, while the man watching grew greedy for gold, and impatient at this delay. When on the third day snow fell, he pulled off your father's blanket with a withered hand.

" 'You'll soon be buried decent all right,' he said. 'You'll have a nice white shroud better'n this old blanket.' Then he stole your father's rifle, too, and his knife and flint, and left him to freeze to death."

Peter felt the hairs on the back of his spine prickle. In a cold flash he saw Lefty Slade riding into the shop on Lucia, with Domingo tagging along. "The withered right hand," he said aloud, unbelieving.

"Perhaps, Peter, I should have told you this long ago, but

I felt you were too young to know there are such vile men. And I couldn't bear to see you become bitter like your father."

Peter heard harsh breathing. He listened, knew it was he himself breathing so heavily. He asked, "How did Pa get help?"

"With his horse gone and his legs useless, he clawed and crawled with his hands, dragging the rest of his body along like a paralyzed thing. He lived on dried buffalo berries and chokecherries, and one night he watched a wolf kill an antelope, and when the wolf had feasted, he ate some of the raw meat and tore off all he could to carry with him. He crept almost five miles before he reached a prospector's cabin."

Peter put his hand in hers, and she lifted it to her cheek.

"Can you imagine, Peter, the aching for revenge that must have wracked him all those long miles?" She freed his hand when Dice objected, stroking the dog's head.

"Afterward," she said, "as soon as your father was able to stand, all he wanted to do was practice target shooting. He used an old skull, and I knew what went through his mind with each shot. I've watched him shoot six times in succession and hit his mark, even at a hundred yards."

"I know. I saw him snuff out a candle with one try."

"Of late, haven't you noticed how he has stopped all this target practice? So you see he *is* improving. I think it was the night he traded Kate, the old white mare, for Domingo's mother that made him feel avenged—without actual killing. His broody silences, however, have not changed. Nor his philosophy, which remains: the strong will survive; the weak shall perish."

"But Ma! I didn't *want* to crack my ribs. Why did Pa call me chicken-livered and shame me in Mr. Brislawn's eyes?"

"You must try to understand, Peter, why he has been severe with you. He wants you to become strong enough and wise enough to face life as it is.'"

"But how could he trade my own Domingo?"

"He honestly believes that in time you will love the big-going Thoroughbred, Galloway, more than Domingo. He even quoted from the Bible. 'When a boy is fourteen,' he said, 'he should put away childish things.'

"Of course, you and I know that no animal can ever take Domingo's place in your heart. But perhaps there is room for loving another in a totally different way?"

The question went unanswered.

"Men fear your father. They respect his courage, his marksmanship, his tradesmanship. They are awed by his violence; some even respect the strength of his violences. But they do not love him, because he himself has forgotten how to love. They avoid contact with him as if he had some dread disease. By the men who know him, he is feared a great deal more than the Almighty. And I, too, fear him but can understand."

Mrs. Lundy wrapped her shawl closer. "Can you forgive him, Peter, knowing why he is trying to make you strong?"

Peter had no idea how long he stood mute, nor when his mother left to go back to the house. He was shocked by this glimpse into his father's past. He wondered what he would have been like in his father's place. He wondered if his father ever tried to imagine himself as a boy again.

When finally Peter did go home, Grandma's black peppercorn eyes went suddenly bright when she saw him. She reached into the folds of her skirt, found the pocket with the peppermints, and held out two pink ones on her trembling hand.

Accepting the simple offering, Peter silently shed his tears. He knew he had forgiven his father.

Part III. The CRUCIBLE

The Handbill

HIS NAME is Peter Lundy and he is one day short of fifteen. He still wears his hair in twin braids, like the Sioux. The fact that his are yellow makes no difference to him, or to the Indians. They still call him Yellow Hair or Little Brother, as does Adam.

The year is 1860. The month March. The day Wednesday, the twelfth. Tomorrow, on the thirteenth, he will be fifteen.

"A man can age years in a day," he thought, as he stood behind the counter of Jethro Lundy's Trading Post. "That is, if he sets himself to it." The dream didn't stay long, being nipped off by a grizzled trapper who threw a pack of beaver skins on the counter.

The trapper ran a broken fingernail through the thick softness of the undercoat. "Ever see such beauts?" he asked. "Worth seven, eight dollars the pound, eh?" He grinned, eyes squinting, testing the boy.

"Sorry, sir. Pa's price is six dollars, and I can't change it."
Peter heard his voice crack and suddenly plunge hoarse and
deep. He had to smile at himself, aging so quickly. Even Dice
lifted his head, facing around to see who it was. Satisfied, he
went back to his dozing, head between his paws.

The trapper shrugged. "It don't matter, kid. Six dollars,
or seven. You can bet your neck it'll all be spent come morning."

A newcomer, standing a little way off, watched the weighing of the pelts, impatient for the transaction to be over. He
had a face like a compass, marked with purpose and sureness.
While he waited, he laid a sheaf of papers on the counter,
squaring them into a neat stack. Then he observed everyone
in the store and in the blacksmith area, the way a horse buyer
might look over a string of horses for sale. Peter felt himself
included in the scrutiny.

As soon as the beaver skins and the money had changed
hands, the man stepped up, moving his papers along the counter.
"I'm puzzled," he said, smiling and showing big white teeth
that looked strong enough to crack nuts. "You couldn't be
Jethro Lundy, the proprietor?" he asked. "Or could you?"

Peter liked the man at once. "I'm minding store for two
days while Pa's away," he said.

"My name's Bolivar. But everyone calls me Bol." He offered a hard, lean hand across the counter. "You can, too,"
he said. "That is, if you like."

"Glad to meet you, Mr. Bol."

"You often mistaken for your father?"

"Oh, no, sir."

"Being you're tall as a lodgepole pine, I'd guess it might
happen regular," he said, as if he meant it.

Having no answer, Peter glanced inquisitively toward the stack of papers. The printing and the picture were upside down to him. Instantly Bolivar turned the stack around and handed a copy to Peter.

The boy's eyes moved swiftly over the page. All at once his heart began to bump against his chest. The blood rushed hot to his face.

"I'd be obliged," Bolivar was saying, "if you'd put up several of these so travelers heading west or east would be sure to see them." He peeled off a small batch, placing them in a separate pile. "They'd be noticed best if you tacked 'em eye-high beside your door, going in and out; and two, three in your blacksmith shop. Oh, and some on your corral fence where young fellows stop to gawp."

Peter, still clutching his copy, kept scanning it out of the tail of his eye, not looking straight at it for fear it might be a mirage and vanish right into the wood of the counter. Yet his mind had photographed it whole so that he could, if he had to, recite it from memory.

WANTED, the heading read, **Young, Skinny, Wiry Fellows Not Over 18**. A picture of just such a fellow appeared alongside, like a giant exclamation point. He wore knee-high boots and a wide-brimmed hat almost as big as Brislawn's.

With a quick intake of breath Peter mouthed the next words: *Must be expert riders, willing to risk death daily.* He repeated this sentence, wondering why the printing was smaller, yet the thought bigger.

Then the big bold letters again, and big bold figures, **WAGES $25.00 Per Week**. Already, in his mind, he had collected his first pay and was thumbing through a catalog, ordering a pile of things—a gold comb and brush for his mother,

a hobbyhorse for Aileen, and pounds and pounds of pepper-mints for Grandma. But even in his excitement he was nagged by two words at the bottom of the handbill: *Orphans preferred*. He frowned, and then suddenly he laughed. It didn't say *Orphans only*. It just said *preferred*. And what if he was only fifteen, just? Hadn't Mr. Bolivar taken him for man-grown? And the notice didn't say *not under 16*, it said *not over 18*.

On every count he qualified! At last Brislawn's prophecy had come true. He could hear his voice: "There's a time for some things and a time for all things; a time for great things, and a time for small things."

The time for great things had come! No need for asking, the knowing was sure.

"Hey, daydreamer! How about it?" Bolivar interrupted. "Will you tack up my handbills?"

Peter nodded, still wrapped in his dream. A knot of men had gathered around, reading the handbill aloud. The trapper nosed up to Bolivar.

"Who be you?" he demanded, jangling the dollars in his pocket. "What's all this about?"

Bolivar made sure his voice and eyes took in everyone. "I'm superintendent for the Western Division of the new Pony Express," he explained. "My job is to recruit eighty young men for the company I represent."

"Whoozat?"

"Russell, Majors, and Waddell." The last-mentioned name he pronounced "Wad'dle."

"Huh, huh! Ho, ho!" a white-bearded man roared. "The name's Wad-dell', like farmer in the dell."

"Sorry to disagree, sir, but W.B. himself pronounces it Wad'dle, as in duck."

Everyone laughed as the old man waddled out of the shop, joining in the laughter at himself.

The foolishness ended. The talk quickened. Questions and answers seesawed.

"What do we need a pony express for? Bad news travels fast enough; good news can wait. Besides, we already got the Butterfield Express. They go every week and travel the hull way from Missouri to California in twenty-five days."

Bolivar measured his words, then shot them out with staccato emphasis. "Senator Gwin of California says that is not fast enough. A shorter route from St. Joe, Missouri, along the Platte River, then west across the Sierra Nevada Mountains to Sacramento would save a hundred miles."

"A hunnert miles over what?" the trapper asked.

"Over the Butterfield route—across the Arkansas River, through El Paso, along the Gila River, and over the sandy deserts of the Southwest."

A chorus of "Hmm's" and "Oh's."

"Y'see, the senator wants our company to organize this shorter, quicker service to bridge the gap between Washington and California. Especially now."

"Why now?"

"With the cotton states wanting to secede, and urging California to join them, there's liable to be war if communications can't get through."

A pompous man, using his paunch for an armrest, said with conviction: "I tell ye, young feller, there'll be war anyway."

"Then all the more reason for the Pony Express."

Peter forced himself to listen. He had to remember all the reasons, to convince his mother how much he was wanted and needed.

Bolivar was patience itself, explaining: "There's deep concern in Washington that California might go independent from both the South and the North; and President Buchanan will want to send dispatches flying across country to halt any such notions."

"*Him?*" The pompous objector scoffed. "Not him! That old bachelor settin' in the White House is a hand-wringer when there's trouble."

"Hey, Superintendent!" A man with a cranelike neck leaned over the group, studying the handbill. "What's a message going to cost?"

"Five dollars a half ounce, written on tissue-thin paper."

"*Five dollars!* Why, that's outrageous! I can think o' far better uses for that paper."

Snickering grew into guffaws. Gibes came fast.

"Hurrumph! I'd send a duplicate letter by stage."

"Name me what kind of news is important enough to spend five dollars fer?"

"How 'bout: 'Dear Ma, I'm fine. How're you?'"

The room broke into a boom of laughter. Even so, Peter sensed an undercurrent of concern, as if the Union *could* be torn apart.

"What kind of time do you expect to make from St. Joe to Sacramento?" a quiet man on the fringe of the group asked.

"We're promising ten days."

"In-cred-i-beel!" a French Canadian exploded. "In-cred-i-beel!"

"But is it worth the risk of life and limb to the young riders?" the quiet man continued.

"Or the money risk?" the pompous man added. "Only thing I got to say, Bolivar, your company'll go broke without government help. Someone's got to pay the fiddler."

"Be that as it may, I'm to engage eighty pony boys at once." He pulled out his bull's-eye watch. "Oh, Gemini!" he exclaimed. "I'm due in Fort Laramie by nightfall." Gathering up the rest of his handbills he strode toward the door, Peter and Dice at his heels.

"Bol! Bolivar! Mr. Bolivar! Wait! I want to sign up. I'm coming with you!"

In one leap Adam was spinning Peter around. "Gawblimy, Little Brother!" he cried. "You can't leave Adam for good!"

"Please," Peter implored. "Please, Adam. Mind shop for me. And I'll write you often."

"Cheer up, fellow," Mr. Bolivar said to Adam, "the Express won't be running for a few weeks." He turned to Peter. "I hoped you'd want to join," he said. "But it isn't all that simple. I'll need the full consent of one of your parents. Come, let's see if you can get it."

Orphans Preferred

MOMENTS LATER, when Peter threw open the soddy door, everything was silent as midnight. Aileen and Grandma had rocked each other to sleep, arm in arm. His mother was sitting cross-legged on the floor, hand-drying her hair by the fire. She looked, Peter thought, like the Lorelei in his *McGuffey's Second Reader*.

She was too stunned at seeing the businesslike stranger and Peter's eyes big with excitement to do anything but remain frozen where she was.

"Ma!" Peter whispered, tiptoeing around the sleeping figures and crouching down beside her. "Read this!" He tried to hold the paper at the right distance. "I aim to join, Ma!"

Bolivar, standing awkwardly by the open door, cleared his throat.

Still clutching the handbill, Peter jumped up. "Oh, 'scuse me, sir." Then turning to his mother: "Mrs. Lundy," he said, as if the sound of anything but "Ma" were new to him, "please to make the acquaintance of Mr. Bolivar. He's superintendent for the Pony Express. He'll take me!" In the same breath he added, "Remember, Ma, there's a time for great things . . ."

"And a time for closing doors, and a bit of hospitality," Mrs. Lundy said with a quick smile. She flipped her hair behind her ears and leaped to her feet, her face gone pink with embarrassment. "Let me put the kettle on, Mr. Bolivar," she said. "Tea and a sweet biscuit will take only a moment."

"Thank you, ma'am, but I have miles to go before dark."

"Then at least sit by the table in comfort until I find out whatever has put meteors into Peter's eyes." She took the handbill and swept the room into stillness as she stood reading the few lines over and over again, as if a second and a third reading might tell her more. The only sounds were the purring whispers of Grandma and Aileen and the precise ticking of the clock.

When it struck the hour, Mr. Bolivar could wait no longer. "Your son, here, is so certain you'll approve his being a pony rider that all I need is your word." He smiled, showing his big white teeth.

"My company believes," he went on quickly, "that if the government could get important dispatches to and from California faster, it might be the means of keeping the nation together. As it is, California feels like an outsider, is even thinking of setting up a separate Pacific country."

"Yes, Ma. We could keep the United States from getting un-united."

"And that, Mrs. Lundy, will take fearless riders," Bolivar added.

Peter's and his mother's eyes met, and held. When her answer finally came, it burst like a light in the drab little soddy.

"Jethro Lundy," she said in a hushed voice, "will be very proud of his son."

"And you, Mamma?"

Her lips trembled in a little smile before she could speak. "I'll be so happy for you that I shall sing all the long days from one of your letters to the next."

Bolivar rose at once. His voice was strangely husky as he told Peter to report at Fort Laramie two weeks hence to sign the pledge of allegiance to the United States. "He's just the kind of recruit we want," he said to Mrs. Lundy. "As the handbill says, we prefer orphans, but without a mother like you, Peter Lundy would not be the boy he is."

A little silence came in before he added: "But in all fairness, I must tell you both that in our final selection, orphaned boys will, of course, be chosen first."

• • •

Into late night Peter and his mother talked across the dark, across the partition of flour sacking. Words seemed to stick up in the air, like clothespins on a line.

"You awake, Peter?"

"Yes, Ma. Sharp awake, but dreaming."

"I can't sleep, either. So I'm knitting by the fire, trying to remember . . ."

"Remember what, Ma?"

"Just how did that handbill read?"

Peter's skin ran prickly up the back of his neck. It took all his willpower not to shout at the top of his voice: "The first line said **WANTED**."

"Yes, yes, of course, I remember that; the letters fairly screamed. But the second line?"

"**Young, Skinny . . .**"

There was laughter in her voice. "You certainly fit that description, though Heaven knows I've tried to stuff you with puddings and porridges. What comes next?"

"**Wiry Fellows Not Over 18.**"

"That, too, fits Peter Lundy to a T. And then?"

Peter went on, repeating word by word: *"Must be expert riders, willing to risk death daily."*

"Oh, Peter! *Willing to risk death*—that's the part where I need more faith."

"But, Ma, think about the next line: **WAGES $25.00 Per Week.** *Per week, Ma.* Not per month. And every week I'll be sending off mail orders to the United States. I'll buy jewelry for you and a hobbyhorse for Aileen."

The laughter sounded close to tears as she said, "Write to me instead, little one, by Pony Express!"

Little one! Peter bit his lip at sound of the pet name, yet it warmed him all the same. He crackled the handbill under his pillow to make sure it was still there. Aloud he said, "Only one thing doesn't fit me, and that's *Orphans preferred.*"

No answer came over the flour sacking. The knitting needles stopped clicking. The prolonged wail of a coyote jolted the quiet. "But it does fit," his mother said at last.

Peter sat bolt upright. Even in his linsey-woolsey undersuit he trembled violently. "Pa ain't my Pa?" he asked, trying to keep his relief from showing.

"Yes, Peter. He is. But I am not your mother."

"Ma!" came torn from his mouth. He prayed for some miracle that would take back her words. Instead, her whispering seemed unbearably loud, driven by an intensity that nothing could stop.

"Your own mother," she said numbly, "and my mother

and father all died of cholera on the same day, in the same wagon train bound for Oregon." The story came in a rush now, as if long rehearsed. "You were just a baby, mostly eyes, and a hungry mouth like a bird's; and you had a topknot of yellow fluff. And your name was Peter, like my brother who had stayed back east in Syracuse to be a concert singer."

Uncle Peter! That letter in the chest was for an uncle who wasn't his uncle.

"And I felt alone in the world, and frightened. Until one day your father asked me to hold you in my arms while the wagon train forded a swollen stream." Her voice was no longer impassive. It grew warm and full of memory. "Holding you," she said, "I suddenly felt strong. From that moment you became all the love I had lost. Don't you see, Peter, I needed you more than you needed me? And that's the way it has been ever since."

Peter felt his whole world turn over. His heart made a slow, heavy thump, then beat so fast it hurt him. After a while he heard himself ask, "Did you marry Pa just because of me?"

"No," the Mrs. Lundy who was not his mother said very gently. "Your cradle was another reason. It was hooded against drafts, and the cutout sides were in the shape of birds and flowers, and the wood had all been rubbed and rubbed until it shone. When I found out your father had made the cradle, carving and all, I felt a great tenderness for him, too."

Peter got up out of bed, thudding across the dirt floor to the warmth of the fire where his mother sat, her knitting fallen from her lap. He kneeled down, putting his arms around her, clinging to her for long moments. Then gingerly he kissed her cheek. "Good night, my mother," he whispered.

He went back to his bed, grown older.

The Long Good-bye

TWO WEEKS later, Peter rode out on Bald Galloway for the new Pony Express Overland Mail Office at Fort Laramie. The moon was still shining brightly.

Last night he had told everyone good-bye, very finally, in case he should be killed and never come back. Everyone, that is, except Dice, who was nowhere to be found.

"Him off sulking somewheres," Adam had explained through his own tears, " 'cause he ain't invited along."

Peter hunched his shoulders into the warmth of his jacket. He missed Dice already. A cottontail rabbit twisted and turned on the road ahead of him. Dice would have gone bursting after her, making turnings and doublings as quick as any rabbit-hound.

The morning tried its best to be friendly. A lone star danced in the east and the Platte River played its same tune over and over. Galloway's new shoes struck the hard-packed earth like hammer strokes. Suddenly the horse's ears pricked.

He snorted, shying wildly as if a rattlesnake coiled near. Peter reached for his pistol just as the grasses parted and Dice leaped up, his tail waving in a great arc of happiness. Pacing himself to Galloway's gait, he fell into stride, traveling alongside as if now at last he were in his rightful place.

"Dice!" Peter's voice cracked high, then went deep and serious. "You can't go."

The dog ran around in front of Galloway and sat down abruptly in the horse's path. Peter pulled up short.

Dice continued to sit. His eyes locked now on the boy's face.

"Don't do it, Dice! Don't hypnotize me! Can't you see I'm hurting, too?"

The dog held his gaze steady. "Don't you *want* me along?" he asked plainer than words.

" 'Course I want you, Dice. But there's sure to be a rule against dogs. You'd be stirrin' up trouble, not meaning to. Like just now. With a nervous horse like Galloway, he could've broke a leg."

Peter dismounted and went over to Dice. For a long moment he put his arms around the dog. Then he stood up and mustered all the sternness he could.

"You go home now. Adam needs you. I got to go on alone, account of this is the time for big things."

Slowly Dice turned tail, looking back often to see if the boy had changed his mind.

Peter felt like turning back with him. He was overwhelmed with misgivings. Would Aileen ever play ball with Dice, and stop poking at his eyes and pulling his tail? His mind slipped back to last night. He thought about his mother's forced gaiety, and his father's silence. Was there a flicker of pride in the deep-set eyes, or had an ember in the fire suddenly burned more brightly?

He thought of the scarf Grandma had made for him, all riddled with dropped stitches, and how he had bragged on her knitting as if it were a perfect thing. He was wearing the scarf now. But as soon as he reached the fort, he'd whip it off and stuff it in his saddlebag, loving Grandma no less. She was proud of him, even if Pa wasn't.

He wished the sun would come up and help him forget Dice and home, a little. But all during the winding miles along the Platte, the sun either hid behind Rattlesnake Ridge or was lost in cloud cover.

Not until he stood hesitant within the fort before the door marked "Arsenal" did a great shaft of light shine up the letters into brassy gold. No one answered his knock. Peter looked back at the officer who had directed him. The man nodded. "Knock again," he said. "Alexander Majors concentrates, shuts out interference like a horse wearing blinkers."

Peter knocked again, louder, wondering at his boldness.

"Enter!" a voice from within rolled out strong.

Peter opened the door and stepped into a room lined to the rafters with books and boxes of ammunition. A high-up window framed Laramie Peak with snow patches in its seams. Alexander Majors sat in the full light of the window, working at a makeshift table with sawhorses for legs. His chair was a powder keg.

Peter blinked. Any other man would have seemed run-of-the-mill ordinary in this storage place of a room. But Alexander Majors put Peter in mind of the power and dignity of the buffalo bull. He was bearded brown, like a buffalo, and broad of shoulder. And the planks of the floor trembled as he strode over to a row of kegs, rolled one alongside his desk, and motioned Peter to sit. Then he went back to his table, heaped with papers and a stack of calf-bound Bibles.

"You are . . . ?" His eyes measured Peter, head to foot, braids to boots and back again. His question hung in midair, waiting.

In his new, deep voice Peter answered, "I am Peter Lundy."

Strong, quick hands riffled through a file of letters on the table. "Ah, yes," he said. "Bolivar told me to expect you, and yesterday's stage brought a letter here from Mrs. Lundy." He found the letter, scanned it swiftly and put it back without changing expression.

"Now," he said, making his tone hearty, "a few questions

and then we both can be about our business. First off, your weight. Are you always this light, or have you been starving yourself to fit the qualifications on our handbill?"

Peter laughed without meaning to. "Me starve, sir? You don't know my mother—my stepmother, that is."

The boom of the man's laughter reached every corner of the room. "I had a mother like that!" he said. "But the results were vastly different in my case, as you can see. The reason we want slim, wiry fellows," he explained, "is that riders must maintain an average speed of fifteen miles an hour, which includes time for change of horses, detours when necessary, and meals. So some parts of each route have to be traveled at, say, twenty miles an hour. A horse can break at this pace if his rider is overweight, or jounces in the saddle."

"I'm used to a fast pace, sir. At least I was ... when I had ..."

A sharp knock at the door and a messenger poked his head inside. "Begging your pardon, sir, but the stage heading east is leaving for St. Joe. Any mail to go?"

Mr. Majors indicated a sheaf of envelopes at the far end of the table. Before the door closed, the messenger said over his shoulder, "Bol just rode in with ten pony boys in tow."

Mr. Majors nodded, making no comment.

Peter sat up straighter, trying to look *Wanted*.

"As I was about to say, Peter, we have bought up five hundred hardy horses and are now in the process of selecting eighty experienced riders. Can you honestly rate yourself *an experienced rider?*"

"Yes, sir!" Peter answered in a burst of enthusiasm. "My whole life I've spent with horses. And some mules and oxen," he added to be truthful. "Yes, sir! I'm experienced in riding, and doctoring, too."

"All to the good, Peter. But remember, one never becomes a finished horseman. He is, rather, constantly in the process of becoming a horseman. Trouble can be the best trainer."

"What kind of trouble, sir?"

The friendly eyes sobered. "Being ambushed by road agents or Indians; or running smack into a mob of buffalo. After each such experience—if you are still wearing your scalp—you are more of a horseman than you were before."

The brown whiskers parted and the lips eased into a smile. "Another question, Peter. How do you regard the red man?"

"The Sioux are my friends, sir. Other tribes are not my enemies."

"Good again. I say: respect breeds respect. If the white man would look upon the Indian as the true native American, and himself an interloper, he would soon realize that there is room enough for all in this great country."

Mr. Majors had more to say. "Now to give you a chance to change your mind . . ." He spread the fingers of his left hand and ticked off more dangers with the forefinger of his right. "I must warn you that in spite of swollen rivers, blizzards, dust storms, burning heat, buffalo stampedes, the mail must go through. *On schedule.* Do you understand that, Peter?"

"Yes, sir."

"And yet," the man took a breath, "you must travel without injury to your horse."

Now Peter was sure he would not change his mind. Never had he felt so sure of anything. Here was a man who cared about his horses, as well as the mail.

Alexander Majors rose to his full-maned height. "I can see a herd of questions milling about in your mind. Ask whatever is bothering you."

Peter's question came lightning quick. "How is my horse?"

"Your horse?"

"San Domingo. He was given to me by an Indian chief."

The man did not hide his puzzlement.

"He used to be mine, sir. Now I'm riding your Bald Galloway."

Majors studied his new applicant as if for the first time. "Why, of course! You must be the son of Jethro Lundy of Rawhide Creek. Your blond braids threw me off completely. I declare, how strange is the long arm of coincidence. . . . Domingo is in fine fettle. He allows my three daughters to ride him triple for hours at a time." He put his hand on Peter's shoulder. "A boy who gave up his own riding horse is entitled to more questions. Speak up."

"Sir! Your Thoroughbred is tied to the hitching post right outside. If I gave him back, could I . . . that is, would you trade him for San Domingo?"

In the quiet that followed, Mr. Majors measured his words slowly, thoughtfully. "One day, when you are a father yourself, you will realize why I cannot take Domingo away from my daughters who have grown to love him so dearly. Only a grave national crisis could make me wrest that little stallion from their hearts."

"But *my* father . . ."

Mr. Majors saw the hurt and interrupted. "Your father thought he was giving you the better horse. Money-wise he was, but not bridle-wise." He took Peter's hand and shook it heartily. "Your father must indeed be proud of you at this moment.

"Now then," he said, bringing the interview to a close, "take this pledge out to the central area and study it carefully. If, in all honesty, you wish to sign it, then present it to Bolivar, who has an office down the line. He will give you a route and order out a saddle and pistol for you."

He tucked the pledge into one of the Bibles, and on the flyleaf of the book inscribed with a flourish:

To Peter Lundy
from
Alexander Majors.

"I might add," he said, placing the book in Peter's hands, "that your little stallion's name San Domingo pleased me almost as much as the animal himself. The meaning, 'Holy Sunday,' touched me deeply, for I am old-fashioned enough to believe in keeping the Sabbath holy."

"Take Your Druthers"

THE OPEN square within the fort boiled with noise. Trappers, hunters, gold seekers, emigrants—all were hungry for supplies and talk. Some were bartering pelts, some offering fine tables and chests too cumbersome for the onward journey. Peter glanced about for a quiet place. Several Pawnees squatted on the floor in a row, soberly absorbing the scene. Peter crouched near them. He had to think. What if there was something he didn't believe in? Would he sign anyway? Then he read the pledge straight through. It was like drinking a dipper of icy well water without stopping for breath:

> *While I am in the employ of Alexander Majors, I agree not to use profane language, not to get drunk, not to gamble, not to treat animals cruelly, and not to do anything else that is incompatible with the conduct of a gentleman. If I violate any of the above conditions, I agree to accept my discharge without any pay for my services.*

Peter searched his pockets for a pencil. He looked to the Indians, who shook their heads. But this document was too important to be signed with charcoal or lead; it called for strong black ink and a sharp pen. His glance darted along the closed doors lining one wall until, spang in the middle, he caught a familiar name. BOLIVAR it said in big block letters.

Quickly Peter was up and running, stumbling over moccasins and boots. In an instant he had knocked and was inside a proper office with a desk, and a lamp with the chimney polished bright, and maps tacked neatly on the walls.

Three young men brushed past him on their way out, two looking pleased, one with eyes downcast. Bolivar was calling to the sad one, "Come back, son, when you are older."

Then Peter stood straight and tall in front of the desk. "Mr. Bolivar!" His mind spoke, but no more words would come.

"Great heart and bottom!" Bolivar laughed. "The Lundy lad, as I live and breathe."

Peter heaved an audible sigh.

"And how did you fare with Alexander Majors?" Bolivar asked, knowing already from his looks.

Peter wiped his moist face. "Fine!" he said, starting to add, "Even if he did take San Domingo away," but the thought was sheared off by the bustling activity of Bolivar, opening up another map that crackled as it unrolled, and talking as he set paperweights in the shape of iron horseshoes on all four corners.

"That man Majors . . . he's the best," Bolivar was saying. "No Sunday work for his riders, but pay anyway. And not afeared of the Devil himself. Keeps a promise, too, like he made it to God in person."

Peter knew of a promise unasked; he wished he could go back and ask it.

"Yes, sir," Bolivar was saying. "Back in '57, when he freighted goods for the Army, he told some big-star generals in Washington that he'd offer his head as a football to kick down Pennsylvania Avenue if he didn't supply the Army with every pound needed for its subsistence."

Peter nodded, beyond words.

"And now he's offered his head a second time for the swift completion of the Pony Express." All in the same breath, Bolivar asked, "You signing up?"

Peter stared at a mug filled with goose-quill pens as if his eyes were magnets to pull one out. Before he could say "Bolivar," the man was into the mug, selecting a pen, dipping into the ink, and offering it across the desk. He motioned Peter to a chair, but he was too late.

Peter, still standing, was signing his name, using his Bible for a desk.

"Guess the Bible makes it extra legal." Bolivar smiled, accepting the paper, powdering the ink dry, and using a pen-wiper to clean the pen. Then, very methodically, he untied a pleated paper envelope and riffled through identical squares of paper. Peter could read his lips saying, "H, I, J, K, L." In among the L's went Peter's pledge.

"Now come around to my side of the desk," he said, "and look at this map." He moved the weights slightly so no part of the map would be hidden.

Peter pored over the squiggles of rivers, and the peaks of mountains, and the place-names very solemnly. In a way it was like looking into a mirror and recognizing your own face—blue eyes, yellow braids, and all. Only here it was the lay of the land which he knew so well—the wavy black lines of Rawhide Creek and the big Laramie skirting the Black Hills. A heavy dotted line ran like basting stitches along the North Platte and across to the Sweetwater.

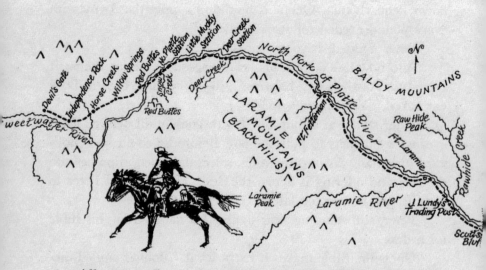

All at once Peter recognized something else familiar. The writing! The o's left open at the top like a hummer-bird's nest, the t's crossed with an upward slash like a unicorn's horn.

"Mr. Bolivar! This looks like Brisley's ... like Mr. Bris-lawn's handwriting."

"It is!" Bolivar's brows lifted in surprise. "No one can make a better map than a surveyor. Do you know that old Irish lepre-chaun?"

"Why, he's my best friend." Suddenly the little man seemed very near, as if he stood in the room, rocking on his heels and chuckling under his big hat.

"Well, he made the map, all right. Of these two routes, Peter, you can have your druthers." Bolivar's forefinger pointed to the dot on Rawhide Creek marked J. Lundy's T. Post. Then his finger traveled east to Scott's Bluff and back west again along the Platte River to Fort Laramie. "On this route," he said, "you could easily live at home."

He paused, waiting for some remark from Peter. When none came he went on. "Or," he said, "you could start farther west at Deer Creek Station, going on through a wilderness of sage to the Little Muddy, and on to the North Platte Station, and over the rolling prairie to the Red Buttes hard by Willow Springs, and on to Horse Creek and Independence Rock, winding up at Devil's Gate. Take your druthers, Pete. I guess it all depends on whether you want to headquarter *with* your family or *away* from 'em."

"Away, sir, please."

Bolivar showed astonishment. "Away?" he repeated.

"Yes, sir."

"With a station keeper, perhaps?"

"That would be fine, Mr. Bolivar. You see, sir, I just found out that my mother is not my mother, and I got to get used to the idea."

Mr. Bolivar didn't see; it didn't make sense to him. Stepmother or real mother, this Peter Lundy was a lucky lad. But he had no time to get into family matters. "Our ranks are about filled now. You can go right on to Deer Creek; that is, if your good-byes are said."

"They're said."

"Good! You'll be headquartering with Maxim Muggeridge, the station keeper at Deer Creek. Maxim's not his real name;

Alexander Majors gave him that handle because the man can't talk without giving out a maxim. You'll soon find out."

"Bol . . ." Peter hesitated, then had to ask. "What's a maxim? Is it something to eat? To read?"

Bolivar chuckled. "It's a pithy saying or a proverb so obvious," he said, "that it hardly bears saying aloud. But Max'll run a fine relay station, and take good care of you and the two or three mustangs in his charge."

He opened a traylike drawer in his desk, revealing several identical pistols. He withdrew one and presented it to Peter. "Keep it always at the ready, son. You may well have need for it."

"I do have one, sir. My mother's. See? It's never been discharged."

"Won't hurt to have two," Bolivar said, examining it with interest. "An experienced horseman can ride without hands. Now, go see the quartermaster, who'll issue your hat and boots." He stood up, shaking Peter's hand warmly. Then impulsively he took hold of Peter's braids and playfully made a noose of them.

"May you keep your hair on your head all the days of your life."

Deer Creek to Devil's Gate

THE MONTH is April. The day Friday, the sixth. Sixty hours ago the first Pony Express rider going west left St. Joseph, Missouri. Now, two and a half days and nine riders later, Peter, at Deer Creek Station, stands ready to take over. He is peering into the distance, trying to pull out of the rolling prairie a horse and rider.

All his last-minute preparations are done, "nice and precise," according to Maxim Muggeridge. Boots waxed against April snow or rain. Neckerchief tied in a square knot. Buckskin tunic belted in. Both revolvers loaded. Bowie knife in boot.

In his mind, Peter flies up the valley of the Platte, skirts the south bank to the North Fork, swims the river to the north bank, strikes southwest to the Sweetwater, past Independence Rock, through Devil's Gate, up the Sweetwater to South Pass, and over the Continental Divide to Sacramento. He's in California, and not even out of breath!

He laughed into the stillness. A sharp pleasure came over

him. He longed to do cartwheels or walk upside down on his hands, but that would be unfitting an expressman. To make the time pass, he rehearsed each creek and hollow of his route, each sandhill and butte. He rode into every relay station: from Deer Creek right through to South Pass and down the west side of the Sierra range—not that he would ever travel such a long route, but it thrilled him just to say the names, and be ready in case . . .

And still no fleck of movement over the swells to the east. Only a finger-streak of light, scouting ahead for the sun. A door slammed behind him, and Station Keeper Maxim Muggeridge, a spare, limping, peppery man with a thatch of red hair, stomped out to join Peter.

"Now, feller," he said, clapping him on the back, "a watched pot don't boil and a watched-for rider don't top outa nowhere. But jest turn yer back, and all-of-a-here he'll be!"

It was an easy thing for Maxim to say, Peter thought, but he felt a growing concern. Maybe he ought to ride east to see if there was trouble. Maybe the pony boy lay sprawled and scalped, and his horse stolen, and the mail spilled everywhere and smeared with blood.

The station keeper noticed the worry in Peter's face. He rummaged in his mind for something to help pass the time. "You ain't asked how I come by the name Maxim," he said.

Knowing full well, but not wanting to hurt the man's feelings, Peter asked without enthusiasm, "How did you?"

"Wa-al, 'twas Mr. Majors pinned it on me, and I be danged if I know why! My birth name's Mallaig Muggeridge. But a short handle, like Maxim or Max, is best remembered. Ho! Ho! Hah! Hah! By any name I smell as sweet."

"Uh-huh."

The gray streak of light was catching fire from the sun. "Once we sight yer partner," Maxim said, making a visor of his hands and studying the empty prairie, "he'll still be several mile away. I'll go saddle up, anyhow. By the way," he added, "either of them other two broncs in the stable'd carry ye faster and further than that Bald Galloway. Oh, well, Majors wants *his* horse to carry the first mail. Only natural for . . ."

He seemed ready to spout another maxim, but Peter interrupted. "I better bridle him; Galloway's head-shy with strangers."

"Humph! The horse ain't livin' that I can't hold. Besides, I aim to save my riders for *their* work. Each cobbler to his last, I allus say." Off he went, hitching his trousers and hobbling toward the stable.

Left alone, Peter tried Maxim's advice. He turned away from the east and faced around at the log-built station. Curls of smoke spiraled from the chimney, blowing white against the red buttes rising bare in the distance. Watching the smoke brought home close. This early in the day the washtub would be boiling and Ma singing in time with the scrub board, and her yellow hair curling from the steam. He suddenly remembered that she wasn't really his mother. Maybe he'd wipe the thought clean away, like you'd brush off a cobweb caught across your face.

From the stable, Max's voice bawled in irritation: "Boy! Get this snorty, spooky, son-of-a-red-devil . . ."

Peter ran to help, feeling the strange thumping of his pistols as he ran. Galloway—still unbridled—alternated between pawing the earth and rearing up, dancing on his hind legs, lifting Max up and setting him down like a puppet on a string. Approaching from the side, Peter spoke to the horse as one gentleman to another. "Fine day, ain't it, friend? Fine day for eatin' up the miles 'tween here and Devil's Gate, eh?"

He took the bridle from Max and moved the reins from Galloway's shoulder up closer to his head, just behind the ears. He held the loose ends snug under the horse's throat. Galloway could no longer toss his head. He waited for his chance, but it never came. The battle lost, he settled down, awaiting the familiar routine. With the bit in his left palm and under Galloway's chin, Peter's thumb and forefingers opened the mouth at the bars while his right hand now pulled up the bridle, helping to guide the bit into place, resting it easily on the bars.

Max Muggeridge eyed each movement. "Wa-al, I be a popeyed bullfrog!" he exploded, too stunned for a maxim.

The faraway drumming of hoofbeats ended all talk. Peter let Galloway curvet out of the stall, and together they ran out to the open place where the mail would be relayed. He walked Galloway in a widening circle, around and around, trying to quiet him, trying to preserve his energy. All at once they both froze. Galloway bugled a high-pitched welcome to the oncoming horse. But there was no answering whinny as Jim Baxter rode in at a gallop, his mount wet-ringed with lather.

In less than sixty seconds Max whipped the mochila of mail from Jim's saddle, swung it across Galloway's, thrust the saddle horn and the cantle securely through the slots. Peter Lundy, the tenth rider of the first Pony Express, was up and away!

The moment had come! Nothing had changed in his world, yet all had changed. He, Peter Lundy, was an unbreakable fiber in a tie-rope that could hold the whole country together, ocean to ocean. He felt awed by the enormity of his task. Galloway, too, seemed to feel the pull of greatness. Lengthening out, he streamed himself into the wind, pounding the plain as if he, too, had a map in his head.

For the first time Peter wondered: why the name "plain"? Hollows and hills pocked and pimpled the land, with here and there fringes of willow to show the river meandering.

To right and left the sea of grass stretched away until the mountains, with their pinpoints of cedar and pine, put an end to it. "Winter's over," Peter thought. A good sign. A good world. "A good day to be alive, eh, Galloway?"

As one creature they twisted and turned with the Platte. They clambered through ravines and over the straightaways, flushing creatures big and small. Ground sparrows and horned larks kited skyward. Prairie dogs, sunning themselves on their housetops, dived into their dens. Antelope bounded into distance.

On through a waste of sage—ten miles of wildness—to the Little Muddy, where a blue grulla mare pawed the earth, waiting to replace Galloway. And now the ford of the North Platte, shallow for April. And the mare splashing swiftly across the half mile of it, fearful for quicksand, and scrambling up the banks as if the Devil and not Time were her goad.

Morning wearing on, and every station entered on time, and a Chickasaw horse ready to replace the blue mare, and later the Chickasaw by a buckskin; some of the horses scuttlers, barely lifting their feet, but swift as wind anyway; and some reachers, like Galloway, with strides spanning a wagon's length.

And the day flying fast as hoofbeats, but things remembered just the same. The lone cottonwood with a dead Sioux warrior lying high on a scaffold under the leafy umbrella, his spear and shield catching the glint of sun. Atop the crown of the tree a bald eagle acted as lookout; and below, a wolf

howled, scratching the bark.

Fast as he was going, Peter thought about the foreverness of death; and life being a race against death but in the end death always winning. He thought about Brislawn, who was closer to death, being so much older, and how Brislawn wasn't afraid to die, only hated the act of dying.

The Indian up there in the tree seemed full of peace; more so, maybe, than when he smoked his long pipe.

Things stuck in the memory. More landmarks to count on

for the road back: this river island wooded, that one bare. An old rocking chair, discarded from a wagon train, tilted in sand.

Press on. Keep going. Carry all the messages unborn, until delivered in California.

And at last the sun grinning behind the jagged teeth of the mountains. Peter's first day done, and night closing in, while the mail goes on over the mountains, and Peter sleeps, curled up in the shaggy warmth of a buffalo robe.

The Scalp-lifters

HOME FOR Peter was now a buffalo robe on the floor of a relay station—either with Max Muggeridge at Deer Creek or with Eli Dogberry at Devil's Gate. It was enough of a home for now.

Peter's first ride was in the nature of a surprise with the tiniest thread of disappointment. The whole first week seemed thinned down from what he'd expected. His interview with Mr. Majors kept flashing in and out of his mind, and he could see the man's fingers ticking off dangers: "Storms. Floods. Rivers swollen. Wolves. Buffalo. Hostile Indians. Bandits." Where were they?

Not that Peter *wanted* the mail threatened, or his own life. He could hardly put a name to how he felt. And then Max Muggeridge did it for him, on a quiet Sunday when they were mucking out stalls. Between forking and pitching Max said, "Bein' a station master ain't 'zactly what I expected."

"No?" Peter stopped work, resting on his fork.

"No, siree! 'Live on expectations,' my pap used to say, 'and one thing's sartain.' "

"What's that?"

" 'Disappointment.' "

Peter listened sharply.

"Station tending's the draggiest work I ever done. I like to be busier'n a handcuffed man with the seven-year itch." He slapped his horse on the rump. "Move over, Bucephalus." And in the same breath, "Never any excitement around here. Nothin' ever happens. Just ready the horses and wait. Ready 'em and wait. Wait, wait, wait seems all I ever do. A feller can't even catch himself a mess of catfish or shoot a buffler. Everything's brought in by wagon train. Now take you. You're lucky. On the move every dang moment. Seein' the world."

"Max," Peter said, "my work's not draggy, but . . ."

" 'Course 'tain't."

"But where's the danger in making all the crossings without swimming? The weather's fine as silk for April, and a fresh horse every few miles, and Cheyennes and Sioux and Arapahos all friendly and saying 'How?' No bandits to kill, no wolves snapping at our heels, no buffalo coming even close."

Max threw back his head and howled. "Well, if you ain't the craziest! Wantin' to look a cannon in the mouth!"

"I guess it's a guilt feeling I have. That's it! *Guilt!*" His own word took Peter by surprise. "I'm not earning my money. You see, I agreed to *risk death*."

"Well, I be dogged! Ain't it dangerous gallopin' full tilt ten, twelve hours a day, jouncin' on a hard saddle?"

"It's more like play, Max. Like when I was a boy, and no goal but hunting an old Indian medicine wheel, or going swimming. Only . . . only then I was riding San Domingo."

"You a mite homesick, maybe? For home, and a horse you give up?"

Peter didn't answer for a while. When he did, "Maybe," was all he said. Then after a pause, "But I didn't *give* him up," he said, his voice lingering long on the word "give."

There was no going home now. No time for it. Rest days were busier than other days. Stalls to muck out. Horses to doctor. Pistols to clean. Clothes to wash. And Max quick at thinking up new chores when regular ones were done.

• • •

Almost from that day of confiding, things began to happen, as though some overall hand was squeezing the trigger, one–two–three, on trouble. The meek gentleness of April gave way to violence. Lightning slit the skies. Thunder rocked the earth. Creeks and rivers swelled and spilled brown water over their banks. Clawed by debris, the horses had to fight the rushing current. Peter fought with them, knees angling them across, voice shouting them across, hands dropping the reins, holding the mochila on high, protecting the mail. For that week of flood Peter felt he'd earned his twenty-five dollars.

On a morning soon after the rains had gentled and the winds were again blowing softly through the grassed hill country, Peter, riding a fast-footed sorrel, noted a small herd of buffalo on the side of a knoll some distance away. Right on schedule the sorrel burst up and over the crown of the hill, expecting to fly down a long, quiet valley. Instead, the valley was all buffalo! Acres of buffalo! Wave on wave of brown wool and horns and churned-up dust! "They're peaceable, though," Peter told himself, "not running, not charging, just drifting slow, and leaving gaps wide enough for a dozen horses to angle through."

In his eagerness to make time, Peter spurred the sorrel too close to a bull. The great lumbering beast let out a bellow of alarm. Instantly a roar of answering bellows echoed up and down the valley. Cows and calves, bawling in confusion, began closing off the gaps Peter had counted on.

Buffalo-wise, the sorrel took over. Like a boxer sparring he zigzagged in and out—twisting, doubling back, swerving, spinning on his hocks, reading the minds of the bulls, anticipating which way the herd would turn. A dozen times he bored a hole through the milling mass, until at last he and Peter were out in open country again.

This was near-danger! This was what Mr. Majors had promised! "I'll write Ma how exciting it was," Peter thought. "She'll be proud of me, but Pa'll know I was riding a buffalo-wise pony."

Max Muggeridge seemed as happy as Peter over the buffalo experience. "Now," he said, "you've had yer flood, and yer buffler. What next? Injuns? Danger's like mice, y'know. Where there's one, there's three."

Peter forgot Max's maxim. He hardly counted the change in the Indians' attitude an out-and-out danger. Besides, they were still friendly to him. If there was a change, it had to be the fault of mosquitoes. In the split second it took to mount a horse, swarms of mosquitoes attacked face, neck, belly, and legs, making the creature spooky and irritable. Mr. Dogberry wiped his horses with citronella, but it wore off before the ride was half over. Then the pesky things came on more savage than ever, sneaking into nostrils and ears, driving the animals crazy.

Yes, if anything could make man or beast ornery, mosquitoes could be the culprits.

Will Cody and other pony riders came up with various reasons for the sullen mood of the Indians. Will thought it was the day-by-day push of the emigrants—spoiling the land, killing the buffalo, trapping the beaver, fouling the streams.

Max, however, was more emphatic. "No!" he said with authority. "A cow's the cause."

Peter had just settled himself into his buffalo robe on the floor and lay looking at but not commenting on the foreboding sandbags piled up against the lower half of the window.

"Come next week, I'm getting a hostler to help," Max announced. "I writ Majors I wanted a feller with a nose like a coyote's so's he can scent Injuns a mile away."

Peter laughed. "I thought you didn't want any helper getting in your hair."

Max's hand flew up, patting his thick thatch. "Now it's different," he said. "No scalp-lifter is going to fleece me o' my crownin' glory—not if I have to hire me a dozen assistants with a dozen rifles."

Peter got up to swat a mosquito. "Cheer up, Max," he said, "it's these pesky mosquitoes that's rankling the Indians. Maybe we'll have a freeze and they'll die off, and the Indians'll be friendly again." His tone was beginning to lack the confidence of his words.

"Mosquitoes, me eye! They fret me, too. But you don't see me goin' around burnin' buildings and raidin' corrals and liftin' people's scalps like they was buffalo chips."

Max produced a wedge of berry pie from under a domed lid of paper and cut it into equal slices. "The real cause of hostilities," he said, offering a piece to Peter, "is due to a cow with a full udder of milk." Chewing and gulping, he relished both the pie and his sermonizing.

"It's all clear and plain to me. The Blackfeet Injuns stole this milker cow from the U.S. Army. A rattle-headed lieutenant demands the life of the Injun. His tribe refuses to give him up. So the Army opens fire, leavin' a lot of Blackfeet spraddled and dead."

Peter's appetite was suddenly gone. He slid his pie back under the paper and went to bed.

• • •

Whatever the reason, the month of May marked the change in the Indians' attitude. Pony riders and relay stations became their target. Cheyennes, Sioux, Blackfeet all wanted horses and firearms—enough to fight the whole United States Army.

On Tuesday, the fifth of June, a station close to the California border was robbed of four horses, a half-dozen rifles, and enough bullets to wipe out a regiment. The building itself was burned to ashes. On Monday, the eleventh of June, Peter left Deer Creek at noon. He crouched low over his horse's neck, not in fear, but copying the Indian's way. Besides, the faster he flew, the fewer mosquitoes could light on his horse's face or his own. A half-dozen Sioux spotted him along the way, but dismissed him as no more than a magpie in the swim of distance.

Against a head wind he made his first station, the Little Muddy, five minutes early.

At the third station he pulled in twelve minutes early. Today he might set a record. The fresh pony, ready and wait-

ROBERT
LOUGHEED

ing, shot away at full speed. They passed the familiar landmarks along the river—the islands bare and the islands wooded, and the rocking chair still tilted in the sand. Grandma Lundy would have crowed at the crazy angle of it. Yes, the landmarks all there, and his pony pounding past them, ears laced back. Suddenly both ears swiveled, then shot forward, pointing toward the tree, the lone tree with the Indian body on the scaffold.

To Peter's horror the body seemed moving, the head canted. Now, barely thirty yards away, the Indian was up, poised on the scaffold, the eagle feathers in his war bonnet quivering in the wind. Like some trick rider he leaped onto the back of a waiting horse, his rifle aimed at Peter.

As he fled, Peter heard the rifle crack. A bullet hissed by him, pinged into the side of a rock. He turned around, firing his six-shooter again and again. He saw the oncoming figure sway and swerve in his saddle.

Peter's gun was empty! Around a bend in the river, he whipped out his mother's pistol, ready for a life-or-death shootout. But he heard no hoofbeats . . . only his own horse's breath rattling.

That night at Eli Dogberry's station, Peter prayed desperately that the Indian trickster still lived. Peter had never killed a man. If the warrior lay dead, he, Peter Lundy, may have touched off a full-scale war.

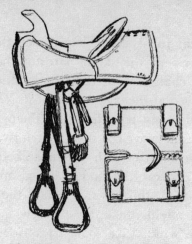

A House Divided

AT FOUR o'clock next morning a courier delivered a message marked for Peter Lundy, care of Eli Dogberry.
"Hope none of your kin be ailing or dead," Mr. Dogberry remarked with gloom as he turned up the oil lamp and pulled over a stool for the boy.

Fear sickened Peter. His hands shook so violently that he had to lay the sheet of paper on the table. In the pool of light he glanced quickly down the page to the commanding signature: Alexander Majors.

> *Dear Peter Lundy* (the handwriting read), *The company of Russell, Majors & Waddell is deeply indebted to you for ridding this Territory of a bandit who has been the scourge of the plains for a dozen years and more. The number of innocent victims he has murdered in his greed for gold and fast horseflesh is ten known, though lawmen estimate his slayings at a full score.*
>
> *This varmint (I refuse to call him a man) has used*

many disguises in his nefarious career, posing sometimes as a doctor and sometimes as an Indian warrior. There is no doubt of his real identity, however. Those fortunate enough to survive his dastardly deeds have identified him by a withered right hand. His real name is Eph Slade.

In recognition of your dauntless courage, we shall include in your next pay a bounty of fifty dollars ($50.00).

Yours very truly,
Alexander Majors

Peter broke out in a sweat of relief. His teeth chattered as he said to Mr. Dogberry, "Now *I* got a letter to write."

Still in nightcap and shirt, Mr. Dogberry scrabbled around in the cubbyhole at the side of the fireplace for pen, ink, and paper. When he came back to the table, he hovered over Peter's shoulder, trying to make out what the important-looking letter had to say. "Bad news?" he asked expectantly.

"No. Here, you can read it. But please . . . I got to be left alone to write."

Mr. Dogberry took Majors' letter over to the firelight while Peter painstakingly began his own.

Dear Pa,
You will likely hear about my killing a man. I didn't know it was Lefty Slade that I fired at. I took him for an Indian playing a trick on me. I am glad it wasn't an Indian.

I guess you would like to think I avenged you, paying back the man who left you to die. But it wasn't that way. You should know the truth, even if you don't like me as much. Ma will understand how it was.

Your son, Peter

He inserted the word "loving," erased it, and was half glad when it showed through anyway. Then he read over the letter once more while Eli Dogberry made a great to-do, stirring yesterday's mash and muttering imponderables to himself.

By the time Peter had pulled on his boots and downed his breakfast, the night expressman came riding in, and Peter went galloping out on a fresh horse, his letter for Jethro Lundy left behind for the slow stage that would stop at Rawhide Creek.

Earth and sky were parting in a ribbon of grayness as he and his mount took off. Strange, Peter thought, how one day a person could feel high-spirited—laughing and sparring and scuffling with the other riders. And the next day that same person became a killer. The word shot terror into him, as if he were the killed and the killer both. He felt suddenly old. Killing was hard on the soul.

• • •

The death of Slade marked a milestone for Peter. Before, he had looked upon himself as a pony boy, riding the clock around, accountable only to his employer, Alexander Majors.

Now he felt laden and involved—not only with what went on in the Nebraska Territory he lived in, but with what went on in the country as a whole. Perhaps this new, deeper concern was part of growing up, of realizing that whatever affected men in high places sifted right on down and affected everyone, including himself.

The messages he carried east and west were no longer anonymous words shuttling back and forth to anonymous people. They burst into life with momentous consequences.

On May 18, Jim Baxter shouted the news before he tossed over the mochila that held it: "Abraham Lincoln's nominated for president!"

Peter felt a satisfaction he could not define. A man who stood up for freedom for everyone must be a kind of prophet, like Moses. Yet in the days that followed, Peter heard nothing but doubts that Lincoln would ever become president.

"He'll never in the world make it!" a traveling tinker announced. The man had invited himself for "a bit and a sup" with Max Muggeridge. Through a full mouth of rabbit stew he spouted: "Such a plain, homely man don't stand a chance against a slick whopper-jawed talker like Stephen Douglas."

Max scratched his head in uncertainty. "I hear tell that Lincoln's voice is on the screaky side."

Peter bristled. He knew how it was to have a high voice when all your thoughts ran deep and strong. "What if his voice does screak?" he asked hotly. "Maybe it carries!"

Often as Peter rode he repeated Lincoln's words: *A house divided against itself cannot stand . . . this government cannot endure half slave and half free . . . it will become all one thing, or all the other . . . .*

"Did the tough little mustangs," Peter wondered, "ever give thought to their role in history? Or did they just live in a routine of happiness—flying from one corral to the next; always finding hay and grain aplenty; and water, sometimes good and sometimes tainted with alkali, but always wet; and sometimes a patch of grazing if the time of year was right?"

Red roans and blue. Buckskins and paints. Copperbottoms and steeldusts. All pressing on. To what goal in their minds? To save the Union? Or to fill their stomachs and rest their bones?

The year circled on. Days melting into weeks. Summer coming in sluggishly with grass drying to nothing, and horses hoofing up furrows of dust, and sun burning Peter's face Indian-brown and bleaching his hair to straw.

And autumn blowing. Goldenrod taking over for wild roses. Cottonwood and aspen flaming yellow. Wild plums sweetening. Geese honking to their winter haven.

And winter with winds lashing like bullwhips. And Peter riding with lungs on fire until he remembers to mask his face with Grandma Lundy's muffler.

Weeks and months going by, with no reply from Pa, but letters from Ma regular as sunrise. *Dice eats with us, but sleeps with Adam. For days after you left he wouldn't eat at all. He's fine now.* Sometimes her letters broke off short, as if someone had said, "Writing again? To that boy!"

By night and by day Peter rode, knowing every bend in the Platte and the Sweetwater, memorizing the boldest names carved on Independence Rock. Someday he might even carve his own there.

Meanwhile, history, relentless, is in the making:

NOVEMBER 6, 1860
Abraham Lincoln wins the election to the presidency.

Peter rejoiced. He thought back to the traveling tinker's scorn of the homely man with the screaky voice. Here was proof that what a man said was more important than the voice that said it.

DECEMBER 3, 1860
President Buchanan's last message to Congress.

Before the headline reaches California, pony riders filter the news: "Buchanan's on both sides! Tells the North that the South has no right to secede. Tells the South the North is to blame by constantly criticizing slavery."

DECEMBER 20, 1860
South Carolina secedes; declares the Union dissolved!

By February 4, five other states had joined her, set up a separate nation, and elected Jefferson Davis their president. "We hope thus to avoid war," their leaders said.

Life, troubled, goes on for the Pony Express. Ride. Dismount. Mount. Ride. Gulp your food. Wash it down. Mount. Ride. And bone tired, sleep. But history never sleeping. History moving faster, sharper.

In his own handwriting Alexander Majors sent a new pledge for each rider to sign. Peter read the single sentence— *I swear true allegiance to the government of the United States in this, her hour of crisis.* He signed with earnest zeal.

JANUARY 29, 1861
Kansas admitted to the United States. Kansas no longer a territory but a full-fledged state . . . a free state with the people prohibiting slavery.

MARCH 4, 1861
Abraham Lincoln inaugurated the 16th President of the United States.

That very night, while Lincoln slept, a copy of his Inaugural message, wrapped in oiled silk, left St. Joseph by Pony Express. On March 6, at four in the morning, Peter stood ready at Deer Creek Station. At four-ten an exhausted rider slung the sweat-soaked mochila across Peter's saddle and panted his instructions: "It's got to be in California in seven days instead of ten."

"Easy done!" Max Muggeridge declared as he slotted the mochila in place. "You're early! Pete's a fly-weight! And

Lucky's a new arrival, fresh as the morning dew. Lucky in more ways," he added with a wag and a wink, " 'cause he's the only animal I got left."

Ears plastered back, Lucky bounded forward at a wild gallop as though some devil were jabbing a sharp-pronged fork at his buttocks. He traveled so fast that the grass flattened from the wind he stirred. But fast as he was going, Lucky read his rider's mind and changed his own. If speed was what the boy wanted, he'd kick and buck instead. In midstride he leaped twisting into the air, jolting Peter forward, then kicking out, wrenching him fore and aft.

"I'll ride the bucks and twists out of you," Peter gasped, keeping the bronc's head up and gluing himself deeper in the saddle. Through buck after buck, Peter stuck on and won the battle. But Lucky had a subtler trick in reserve. He quieted down to a walk, slow enough for a funeral cortege.

Peter clucked in vain. He urged with thigh, knee, calf, voice, and finally spur. This was the crisis where the safety of rider and horse was secondary to the need for speed. But even with the spur, the big head only nodded and the pace slowed. For the first time, and of all times, Peter had drawn a rebel!

Frustrated, he jumped off and for a mile he ran the hills up and down, as if to show Lucky how it should be done. Winded at last, he made the horse stand still and, holding the reins taut, he remounted just as a rider topped the next hill with two horses on a string. Peter eyed them longingly, while Lucky shot forward, eager to nose his fellows.

"Peter Lundy!" the rider shouted. "Bless my heart and bottom."

"Bolivar!" Peter sang out in relief. "Is one for me?"

Bolivar laughed his great laugh. "No, siree! I'm delivering fresh horses, replacing the dead, the stolen, and the wore-out ones. These are for Muggeridge. His corral's empty."

"I know! I know! I got this outlaw from him. He won't go unless he sights a relative."

Bolivar wheeled his string alongside. "He's got a mean eye, he has. We'll double back and race you into your relay station."

With Bolivar and his horses setting the pace, Lucky followed eagerly. The wind streamed back, carrying Bolivar's words in staccato snatches. "California's teetering on the brink . . . . Could go to the South. Or could form a new Pacific Republic."

Silence as moments and miles sped by. Then more snatches. "Lincoln's message has got to get to California . . . lightning fast! He's counting on the Pony to pull California back into the Union. You're riding against time, Pete."

Bolivar pulled off the rutted trail. "We're leaving you now. You can see Little Muddy Station and a dandy horse waiting." He headed east with his string, a secretive smile on his face.

Even for a mustang, Peter thought, the horse at Little Muddy looked smaller than most. He had hoped for a stouter one; but anything would be better than Lucky.

As he rode up, two hostlers almost ripped the mochila out from under him. "You're late!" they said, surprise and accusation in their tone.

A gust of March wind lifted the mustang's forelock. Peter smiled in anticipation of a good ride. Here was a Medicine Hat, a new one to the Pony Express. He was bound to be an improvement over the rebel; that is, if he was anything like San . . .

Peter's heart began pounding against his ribs. Time was suddenly of no matter. Slowly, cautiously, he made his feet inch forward—one step and another.

He heard, yet he didn't hear, the hostlers' chatter; it was drony as fly buzz. His inner self was arguing very distinctly:

"*There are other Medicine Hats in the world, you know, besides* him."

"I know that."

"*Why, Lucia could have had several colts by now. Domingo could have fathered a few, too.*"

"But would they be marked exactly like him?"

"*Why not? They call it prepotency, don't they?*"

Peter ran his hands down the inside of the pony's forelegs. They were clean and utterly smooth. No callous patches! None at all!

When he stood up, the horse sneezed in his face and the spume of it spattered the boy. He threw back his head and laughed to the world. It *was* Domingo! Alexander Majors had kept his word. The grave national crisis had come!

How simple was their reunion! Not a word spoken, but everything said in quivering snorts and murmurings; and brown velvet eye talking to blue laughing one.

In a split second Peter was aboard before the dream could break apart. The two creatures were flying west as gray morning burst open with sunlight, Peter fearing his own heart might do the same.

War Paint

FOR THE next fifteen miles San Domingo, the Medicine Hat stallion, had to scorch the plains, making up the time Lucky had lost. "I should be happy enough," Peter told the swiveling ears, "to be with you for fifteen miles, without asking for forever. But wishing's easy." Now they were together again, Peter resolved that somehow they would make up the lost time of being apart.

For two miles they raced through sunlight and sage without slacking pace. Only two miles more to the bridge over Snow Creek, then eleven to North Platte, the end of Domingo's run. If it weren't for the Inaugural message, they could lag along in easy, lazy lopes. Yet, Peter reasoned, burning speed and a record broken might keep Domingo in the Pony Express, and never again in Majors' corral.

Halfway to the bridge a mule rabbit bounded onto the trail a hundred yards in the lead. It seemed unable to turn off, away from pursuit. Terrified by the nearness of Domingo's hoofbeats, it held to the trail, skimming the earth, hopping along in kangaroo leaps, hopelessly trapped by its own fear. "Dare we veer off and break stride for a jackass rabbit?" Peter thought. "Lose precious seconds for a dumb critter without sense enough to dart into the tall grass?"

No need to decide! The trail takes a sharp right turn, up an incline and onto the bridge. With its one-track mind the rabbit keeps arrow-straight ahead, thrashes into the brush and almost tumbles into the creek! Free in spite of itself!

Peter laughed. This was like old times, chasing rabbits or flap-winging birds.

On the other side of the bridge a wagon train of Mormons —men and women dragging handcarts—stopped and pulled off the trail, waving Peter a come-on filled with awe and admiration. A fleck of foam from Domingo's mouth landed on the cheek of a small boy in the group. Peter saw the boy's hand fly up to cover it, as if he would never again wash the face that had almost touched the Pony Express.

Seven miles more, up the valley of the Platte. Sun friendly for March. Stream flowing swift. Peter mulled as they sped on. With other horses on other days he would cross over from the south bank to the north by ferry. But today was *today*. Take the faster way. Who minded cold water and whirlpools and quicksand when time gained could mean a state gained for the Union?

Ford the river! Save the time! Domingo, willing, rips a path through the brown water, swerving to avoid sink holes, feeling his way over the gravelly bed, swimming when he has to. Then lunging for footing up the black, oozy mire of the far bank. The mochila dry, the message safe, and North Platte Station looming ahead.

Peter let go the reins and yanked out his watch. Domingo had covered the fifteen miles in forty-eight minutes; he'd made up for Lucky with minutes to spare!

Cumulus clouds were throwing patterns of light and shadow over the log building as they thundered into the station. They pulled up into a world of silence, broken only by feeble cries, like the yipping of a prairie dog.

Peering out from behind a greasewood bush, Peewee, the young hostler, stopped whimpering. Crouching, stumbling, he came forward, his face old and ashen. "He's dead!" the boy wailed, pointing to the dark silence of the station. " 'Rapahos done it! His ears cut off. His scalp's gone. And his innards . . ." The boy's eyes went wide in horror. "Go look, oh, go look for yourself."

"You certain he's dead?" Peter asked.

The boy bit his lips, nodding.

"No need to look, then." Peter's gaze traveled to the empty corral, to the water buckets overturned.

"They catched our horses," Peewee blubbered. "They chased 'em off with theirn. And they was laughing loud and crazy. And I hid in a hole behind the bushes and then . . ."

"Stop it, Peewee! Climb aboard. We'll take you on to Red Buttes. You can't stay here alone."

"Oh, no!" the boy cried out. " 'Rapahos gone that way. I'll get kilt!" He scurried back to his hideaway, whimpering again, the same feeble, prairie-dog cry.

Peter threw his pouch of jerky in Peewee's direction, spun around, and galloped out of the clearing. There was no choice but to go on, Domingo tired or not. He thought about the station keeper, the French Canadian, lying back there dead and mutilated. Killing ought to be enough, but he knew the

Indians' fear of a dead man's returning to life, strong as before and avenging himself; that is . . . unless his body had been cut to pieces beyond use.

In the brassy sunlight Peter and Domingo dashed on. In every shape that rose on the plains ahead Peter saw Indians with spears ready, bows drawn. They seemed giants, ten to twelve feet tall, with headdresses wide as eagles' wings and long as chimney smoke. Their horses, too, stood tall, their heads sawing up and down, raking the clouds. Yet Peter was only a little afraid. He knew he was seeing a mirage, and the superstitious Arapahos avoided the place of mirages.

To calm himself, he traded talk with Domingo. "Remember Brisley?"

The pounding hoofs were answer enough.

"Knew you did. Well, he said a Medicine Hat's sacred. Neither rifle ball nor arrow can harm his rider. Guess your war bonnet and shield can cast a spell stronger'n Injuns' charms and spells."

As they sped on in the lone emptiness, the mirages grew more beautiful. The cloud-raking ponies were mirrored in lagoons of purest water. Manes tossing, they pranced and plashed, sending up fountains of crystal. But when Peter and Domingo caught up with the scene, the horses had smalled down to little foxes, the giant Indians were clumps of sage, and the lagoons had dried into crusted ponds of salt.

"Domingo!" Peter shouted. "Do you see mirages, too? You must! Else why, 'way back there, did you pull toward the shimmer of water?"

Recklessly they traveled onward over the bare, flat plains and the hills up and down. Peter's mind began picking worries from hearsay. "I've heerd . . ." Was it Adam's voice, or was it Max's saying, "I've heerd of whole bands of water-starved cattle chasing from one mirage to the next 'til they died of exhaustion."

He urged Domingo to full speed, explaining, "At Red Buttes there'll be real water, and rest for you while I go on." He lapsed into silence as they raced through a long valley to its end, then climbed steep hills and ridges, each one sharper than the last, toward the foothills of the Red Buttes and the bold, jutting knobs beyond.

"Domingo, the station is there! You've done ten miles in thirty-five minutes!"

Peter listened anxiously to the horse's breathing. He was blowing, but normally. Relieved for the moment, he let his own muscles relax. He hadn't hurt Domingo's heart or wind. "Those girls of Mr. Majors," he thought, "must've exercised him just right."

As they turned into the clearing of the station, Taggart,

the keeper, came running out, shouting, "Don't stop! Go on! You'll save time!"

Peter ignored him. He jumped down, loosened the saddle. His voice showed sudden anger. "Domingo needs water, needs cooling out. He's done two routes already."

"He's got to do three. We've been raided; our horses are gone. And ye're carryin' the Inaugural."

" 'Rapahos?"

"No! White emigrants run 'em off. They're scared pea-green of Injuns on the warpath and want faster horses."

Peter knew what he had to do. He knew he wasn't just a boy with a pet pony. His mount was an Express pony.

Two helpers came running out, carrying water and a fresh saddlepad. "We'd of been ready," one said, "but we thought you was going right on."

"My blame," Taggart admitted. "Figured any pony could do two stints. Didn't know yours was spent."

"*He ain't spent!* He just needs a little water and time for a breather."

Domingo drank noisily, objecting when Peter pulled the bucket away, rationing the water, a few sips at a time. Between gulps, Peter washed Domingo's face with the coolness, and washed up over the red-brown bonnet. Then his legs. "I guess everything depends on you, Domingo." A few more sips and Peter was cinching up, springing into the saddle, galloping off.

"Keep yer eyes peeled!" Taggart called after him.

The trail now struck out from the Platte River over drear, bald, never-ending wilderness. Not a tree for concealment. Only loneness and desolation.

Peter ran ahead in his mind, putting a name to landmarks: Poison Spider Creek, a dry, broken crack in the earth that once, maybe, held bluegills and chub, and once-watered green grass that was now dry and sticking up from the blistered earth like pinfeathers. He felt Domingo's muscles slacking, tiring, felt him slow, then suddenly tense in response to buzzards heading for a mound of death. Race the buzzards there, leave them there, picking bones already picked clean.

Go on and on, up and over and down, clattering over the ruts, over the sandstone ridges. Shortcut the trail, climb Devil's Backbone up and up to the eagles' aerie. Stop there for Domingo to blow. Dismount to ease his back. Give him time. Don't listen to that other self nagging: *"You're slacking, violating the pledge to your country!"*

Up there on the crest Peter cried, "No! No! No! Domingo'll go faster for the resting."

And his inner voice still prodding: *"How'll he go faster, down those steep crags that break horses' legs?"*

"I'll give him his head, that's how." He shouted that other self down. "I'll let him pick his own way."

To Domingo he spoke Injun-soft. The stallion sensed danger, and terrible urgency. He snorted the breath from his lungs, sucked in a fresh gulp of air, faced the plunge down Devil's Backbone. "Climb aboard," he said, more plainly than if he had talked. "I'm ready."

Peter sprang up, his weight now far back. Domingo tensed, crouched on his haunches, began sliding down, hind legs tucked under, forelegs propping, braking, releasing, sliding, zigzagging. Seconds, minutes, sweat-filled. Man and horse indivisible.

At the bottom, Domingo gave a long, whistling sigh. He shuddered the dust from his body.

"Only one sprint left," Peter encouraged. "Only one sprint to Willow Springs, and pure water bubbling down from the Green Mountains, where no Injun nor white man can steal it away." He spoke soothingly, his head close to the furry ear.

Ten minutes later, in weary triumph, they rode into the station.

"You're way early!" The keeper and his hostlers cheered.

"We know!" Peter agreed. "Domingo's done thirty-nine miles in two hours and thirty-three minutes. Please cool him out slow."

He lifted the damp foretop and caught his own reflection in the brown eyes. "It's not good-bye, Domingo," he promised. He stood for a moment with his cheek against Domingo's neck. Then with determined heart he mounted a fresh horse and faced west.

Ambush

IN SEVEN days and seventeen hours Lincoln's message reached California, breaking all records of the Pony Express. The people of California—Unionists and Secessionists alike—pored over the words, studying Lincoln's warning: *I give my solemn oath to preserve, protect, and defend the Union. Physically speaking, we cannot build an impassable wall between our states . . . . I hold the Union perpetual.*

In a speech to his legislature, California's Governor Leland Stanford rose to Lincoln's defense: "The federal government is still in existence, with a *man* at the head of it. Our great state will remain loyal to the Union."

Like storm clouds lifted by fresh winds, the rebel groups surrounding Sacramento disintegrated, lost interest in their plans to form a separate Republic of the Pacific.

The message *had* reached California in time. Peter and all the other pony boys who took part in the famous ride felt proud of their help in saving the Union. They rode on, in grinding routine, unaware that the South was preparing for war. Peter lived these days on a seesaw of misery and bliss—misery when he had to leave Domingo; bliss when they met again.

Meanwhile, there was uneasiness in Washington over the unpreparedness of the North. Government forts were poorly protected and supplied. In early April, Fort Sumter, in Charleston Harbor, sent an SOS to Washington for food. By ship and train federal cargoes were rushed to the fort. Mistaking the supplies for arms and ammunition, the Southerners opened fire.

Even then, the pony boys did not expect a full-scale war. They rode on, tossing the mochila from one saddle to the next.

May and June went by. And every second or third day, for a brief hour or two, Peter and Domingo were together again, with no thought for anything beyond their joy in each other and in the living, breathing, singing wilderness.

But on July 21 the United States stopped wearing blinders to the facts of war. Jim Baxter raced into Deer Creek Station, yelling, "Northern troops retreating in the Battle of Bull Run! Lincoln calls for seventy-five thousand volunteers."

The catastrophic news spread like brush fire. Manes and tails now licks of flame. Hoofs burning up distance and time. Alexander Majors no longer saying, "Take good care of your horses." Now the command, "Get full speed out of them."

What amazed Peter was that, while other horses grew gaunt and ribby on this torrent of speed, Domingo thrived, grew tougher. Yet Peter couldn't shake a secret terror that never stopped gnawing at him. It was born of such shame he couldn't speak of it even to Max. The fear kept running around in his head like a mouse in a cage. If the war were suddenly to end, Domingo would be sent back to the daughters of Alexander Majors. Peter couldn't bear losing him a second time.

At thought of it, the old hatred for his father boiled up again, as if the tragedy had already occurred.

But instead of an early peace, the rebellion of the South stiffened, and prophecies of a short war were drowned in blood. Domingo and Peter belonged to this life, belonged to flight, and the fight for their country. No time now to halt the Overland Stage, asking, "Is the way ahead clear of Indians? Of road agents?" No time now to wave to emigrant children.

Only a glance at the surveyors dotting the trail, to see if among them was a little whiskery man, mostly hat. One day Peter pulled up short, his voice a medley of doubt and hope.

"Brisley! Brisley?"

The little man turned, smiling. "I favor him," he said, "but I'm his brother Ferdie."

Peter's face fell.

"You must be his young friend, Peter Lundy," the brother said. "On your day off, you go see him. His shack is only a hoot and a holler north of Independence Rock, plumb near yer next pony stop."

Peter reined around, then came back. "What you surveyin' for?" he asked.

Ferdie shoved his hat back in a gesture so like Brislawn's it made Peter's heart ache. "I thought everyone knew!" he said. "The telegraph's comin' through—all the way from St. Joe to Sacramento. Then it's good-bye and farewell to the Pony."

On the heels of the surveyors came the pole diggers, laughing and singing; then scores of linemen waving gaily from their perches in the sky. As day after day Peter saw the procession of men and supplies, he had hours to think: After the Pony Express, what? Home? The trading post, and Pa? "Please, God," he prayed, "don't let the Pony end. Not ever."

The Indians worried, too. The white man was digging holes in *their* land, stringing wires across *their* sky. Burnings and scalpings were the answer, and rifles replacing arrows. Ronny Fergus, a pony boy, shot dead on his horse while talking to the linemen. Two stations in the Sierras burned to ashes.

Yet Peter's rides remained unmolested. Word had traveled from Sioux to Cheyennes to Arapahos and back again: "Pooty good fella . . . brother to Indian." His Indian ways amused and pleased them—his twin braids tied with thongs; the way he sat on his horse; the way he mounted on the off side, Indian fashion, instead of on the near side, like the white man.

Only the Crow tribe mistrusted the boy with the yellow hair. "Him no Crow," they said. "Him steal Medicine Hat."

One late night with a full moon riding, Peter on Domingo was heading for Devil's Gate, the last station on his run. For miles he had not seen a moving creature. The land was mute, deserted. Not even a rabbit leaped from the sage, nor a coyote or wolf howled at the moon. He felt an uneasiness he'd never known before, as if from every mountaintop and ravine eyes were watchful, boring into him.

For the first time he wished Domingo were dark brown all over, instead of a white target in the spill of moon. He knew every Indian, every outlaw lusted for a sacred Medicine Hat. A feeling of fierce possessiveness took hold of Peter. No one else could have Domingo. Domingo was his! His to save and protect from whips and spurs and wolves . . . from everything that could hurt him. "I know now how a mare feels," he thought, "when a snarling wolf threatens her colt."

Independence Rock was behind them now. Only a few miles until he and Domingo could bed down in the warmth of straw and buffalo skin.

The night deepened. The Sweetwater picked up starlight, and quicksilvered a moon-path. Peter was suddenly afraid. He thought he saw Indian fires at the gap in the rocks of Devil's Gate; or were the moon and the stunted pines playing him tricks?

Ahead, banking the Sweetwater, a row of willows made a long arbor of shade. Even with Indians lurking behind the trees, Domingo would be a lesser target skinning through the tunnel of leaves.

Peter dropped his reins, whipped out his pistol, commanded himself: "Get out of the open! Head for cover!" He tightened his knees. Domingo bolted into the broody willows as if he were in a race for fun. Halfway into the trees a rain of arrows and rifle balls crashed through the leaves from both sides. Peter returned a volley of fire. One arrow grazed his thigh. He barely felt the sting of it, barely felt the whip of branches across his face as Domingo slashed through them.

Out from the tunnel of trees now, and up the slope, the wind fierce in their faces. As suddenly as the terror began, the night went back to silence. Peter's sigh was a high whisper of relief. It hurt to breathe. And still Domingo seemed unwilling to slacken his pace. Almost to the top now. The world all silent and at peace again.

They would stop at the crest to blow, but before Peter could draw rein, Domingo stumbled to his knees. Peter leaped off, watching in horror as his pony fell heavily onto his side. And then in the bright moonlight Peter's eyes caught the spurting of blood and a trail of blood staining the path behind them. With a cry Peter fell down beside Domingo. "I should have stayed in the open, but, oh, Domingo, I thought . . ." He didn't finish the thought.

Desperate, torn by conscience, he pulled off his neckerchief, wadded it into a ball, and pressed it against the ragged hole in Domingo's side. For long seconds he sat holding the crumpled wet thing to the wound. "Domingo," he whispered, "I thought only of the arrow that near killed me when it was you that stopped a bullet."

The pony's eyes were open and amber-lit, and the nostrils fluting, and the ears asking.

"Yes," Peter answered. "I'll be here. I'll stay." He loosed the cinch and tossed the saddle and the mail on the grass. He took off his coat and put the warm side over Domingo's body, tucking it gently about him.

He sat close, in silence, in the cold night while the moon slowly slid down and down into the pocket of the horizon. He tried to make his mind think about the mail, about the men in Washington who had written the messages, and the telegraphers in Washington who had translated them into dots and dashes, and the receivers in St. Joe translating them again into words that now lay sealed in his mochila. He tried to think of the horse and rider waiting at Devil's Gate, and Mr. Dogberry fretting and pacing.

But his mind numbed, and his free hand stroked the divided mane that never would stay on one side of Domingo's neck or the other, but grew in its own sweet stubborn way. In dazed sadness he got up and placed both hands tenderly, like a mother-person, over Domingo's heart. All he could feel were the sweat-dried hairs, and no stirring beneath.

He stayed with Domingo until there was no warmth left in the great body beside him. Then he put Domingo's forelock over the brown hairs of his Medicine Hat, and he let it cover the eyes too, thinking about that long-ago time when the wind had tossed the forelock aside and shown him what manner of colt was his. And he saw him impish and young again, kiting up to Lucia, bunting her for his dinner. And then he thought of Brislawn's words: "He's a Medicine Hat! To the Injuns he's big medicine. He's sacred. A god. Nothing can harm his rider. Not slingstone, nor arrow. Not rifle ball, nor lightning."

He didn't want Domingo to die for him; to give him all he possessed, which was his life. He longed to hear him neigh again and sneeze again. And then the tears flowed and would not stop as he tore up fistfuls of greasewood and sage by the roots and gathered buffalo chips and built a fire to keep the wolves away until he could come back with pick and shovel in the morning.

Then burdened with mochila, saddle, and bridle, he

trudged in the chill morning—hatless, coatless, and with pants torn—the two miles to Devil's Gate Station.

• • •

The next hours were lost to Peter. He remembered nothing of reaching the station or handing over the mail. He remembered nothing until the sun was high overhead and he found himself sitting on the doorstep in the sun, still wearing his blood-spattered shirt and the pants ripped where the arrow had grazed. Behind him he heard the clattering of tin plates and the sizzling of frying meat.

"Soon," Peter told himself, "I will feel strong enough to go back and dig the grave." His tired brain tried to reason: Would Domingo like a carved marker telling of his bravery? Or would he like the earth smoothed over so that only Peter could find the place and never any strange eyes prying? He had about made up his mind when his nostrils smelled dust and the Overland Stage came rattling up to the station, which was not a regular stop.

With much pulling and shouting, the driver halted his horses, jumped down from his box and opened wide the door—for Alexander Majors and the man Bolivar.

Mr. Dogberry came running out and poked Peter to his feet with a kindly, "Mind yer manners, son." Then bowing, he said, "My roast ribs of buffalo are about ready, gentlemen. I'd be honored . . ."

Mr. Majors shook his head. "Thank you, Eli, but my business is with Peter. Then we must continue to Fort Bridger."

"Sir," Peter's words fell heavily, "it was my fault, sir."

"In what way, Peter?"

"I should have stayed out in the open, but I thought . . ."

"Nothing is your fault, Peter. There is a destiny that shapes our ends, and we have little to say."

Peter's misery was past bearing.

"All life is a crucible, Peter. It tests our mettle, sometimes almost beyond endurance."

Mr. Dogberry interrupted. "Begging your pardon, sir, but the boy ain't slept and he ain't et."

"Perhaps you'll try those buffalo ribs, now that you know I don't fault you."

"But, sir, I must get back before the wolves . . ."

Mr. Majors shook his head again. "You won't need to go back, Peter. Bolivar here and two pole diggers dug the grave deep, and San Domingo is lying peacefully inside, and they piled the earth softly atop him and smoothed it while I read from the Book of Common Prayer, 'Earth to earth, ashes to ashes, dust to dust.' "

The stagecoach horses began pawing fretfully, and those in the stables, sensing their presence, let out shrill whinnies. Above the chorus Mr. Majors said, "Now then, Peter, would you like a new route in the faraway Sierras? Or would you like to return home? You've earned a change or a rest, and I should recommend the latter."

A silence fell between them while heads poked out of the coach, listening for the boy's reply.

It came without hesitation. "Sir, I have an old friend who lives only a short way from here and . . ." Peter hesitated, afraid he might burst into tears at the thought of Brislawn.

Mr. Majors finished off the sentence. "Now, if ever, is the time to seek the comfort of an old friend." He held out his hand to Peter, and there was such a wringing clasp between them that Mr. Majors' face broke into a great smile.

They stood so for a long moment.

"Forward Is the Ticket"

TOWARD LATE afternoon on the same day, Peter slowed his steps, then halted. By instinct, by love and need, he had traced the meandering trail through the grasses to Brislawn's shack. He knew at once when he had found the place—not by the neat-built shack, but by the animals in the corral. They all turned his way, staring in statuelike silence. Goats and burros, horses and banty chicks—all seemed in a trance of curiosity. Some Peter had never met before, but those he knew he called to by name.

"Shoshone! Choctaw! Sweet Sioux! Jenny! Nanny!"

The spell broke. Nostrils snuffed and whuffed. Legs slow-footed toward him, then bodies jostled each other in their eagerness.

Peter leaned over the fence, offering both hands to be lipped. Nanny-goat danced forward, toed the top rail eye-to-eye with Peter. Did she, he wondered, see more with the barlike pupils of her eyes than humans with their round ones? A young horse nosed his way between Choctaw and Shoshone. He had one yellow eye, one brown. Peter waved his hand before the yellow eye and was glad when the eyelid blinked.

Somewhere far off, a meadowlark whistled as if he couldn't stop. For a moment the song brought homesickness. Peter turned from the animals and set his lonely heart and aching legs toward the shack.

The latchstring was out. He pulled it and went inside. No one was home. But all in a moment the room engulfed him with the warmth of Brislawn. It smelled sweet of leather and tobacco, apples and wild plums, and chicken stewing in a pot over a banked fire. He ate one of the plums, thick with juice, then fell onto the cot, sinking deep into the dry cornhusks and leaves. Now at last he knew the depths of his tiredness and the beginnings of peace.

A ring-tailed cat leaped up beside him, tentatively whiskering his face, his ears, his hair. Purring her approval, she relaxed, wriggling and squirming against Peter, pummeling him with her boxing-glove paws. Peter no longer felt alone with sadness. His fingers stroked the shiny fur, accepting the living warmth. It was almost like being with Dice, except for the rumbly sound of the purring.

The sun, working its way around the sky, poured a yellow haze over the bed. A great drowsiness flowed into Peter. He blinked, trying to focus on objects in the room—on the map over the mantel, on the surveying instruments in the corner, on a clipping of Abraham Lincoln's Inaugural Address hanging on the wall beside the bed. But the harder he tried to stay awake, the sleepier he grew. His arm fell over the brink of the cot, alongside the dangling tail of Ringtail Cat. Soon both creatures fell into a deep sleep.

Brislawn found them so. In the half twilight he didn't recognize Peter at first. Then he took a step closer and opened his mouth to let out a clarion cry of welcome. But the sound never came. He saw the drawn face of the boy, the weary flush of his cheeks. On tiptoe he turned and steadied his rifle on the antler rack. Carefully he hung up his bullet pouch so it wouldn't bang against the wall. His mind was jumping with questions. "Something's saddened the boy," he thought, making a fist at the person or thing that caused it. "Else why the smear of shadow beneath his eyes? And how come he's so thin, and plumb wore out with fatigue?"

He lighted the oil lamp, shielding it from Peter with a half-circle of tin. Then he set to work, heating water, making a batter of corn meal and lard, stirring the mix. The cat opened one eye accusingly, then purred itself back to sleep.

"Nothin' so bad," Brislawn said to himself, "but what hot corn bread and stewed-hen gravy can lessen the pain." He beat the batter, gently at first, then fiercely when he saw that nothing disturbed the boy.

Minutes ticked by. And the quarter hours. The window was black with night when Peter opened his eyes. Still half asleep, he stared into the fire until he caught movement beside it. And there *he* was! Hat and all! Robert O'Breaslain, son of the Kings of Ireland! For a moment Peter studied the little man in silence, thinking, "He hasn't changed, hardly any . . . only his hat seems a bit bigger and himself a bit smaller." The fire caught the lower half of Brislawn's face, shining up the yellow moustache. Suddenly the hat turned, and Peter saw his eyes underneath had not changed at all! A fierce joy leaped up in him; and such a warmth and happiness coursed through Peter's body that he was across the room like an arc of light. Words caught in the tremble of his throat, but no matter. Brislawn was saying them all, and hugging him like a long-lost son, and cheering loud enough to be heard over the mountains and beyond.

At the sound of the racket, the door burst open, letting in a black dog and a white one and a frowsy pup that barked in high C.

"Peter," Mr. Brislawn said as the three rushed in, "you remember Blacken and Penny, but now make the acquaintance of Penny's last pup, name of Handy Andy Potlicker."

The room grew merry with laughter as Handy Andy lived up to his name, eagerly licking a dish on the floor, already tongue-scrubbed to a shine by Ringtail Cat. Oh, but it was good to laugh again, and no questions asked. No "How'd ye come?" Nor "Why?" Nor "Where's yer horse?" Nor "How long ye stayin'?" Only this tug-chain of happiness tight between them.

Peter stretched in sheer animal bliss before he sat down at the table. Brislawn smacked his lips over the super he'd prepared. "I hate eating by my lone," he said as he took Peter's plate and ladled gravy with a lavish hand over hen and corn bread both. "If it weren't for Blacken and Penny, and little Potlicker here, I guess I'd just dry up and blow away like a tumbleweed. But now you've come," he went on, "and forever long as ye're here, we're going to have prime vittles, with gravy and honey beslubbered over everything."

After supper the talk unleashed. Comforting talk, like balm on a wound. Brislawn reassuring, "No. 'Course ye're not a quitter if you plan on leavin' the Pony Express. Could be ye're thinking way ahead."

"Then it's true about the telegraph takin' over?"

"True as we're setting here."

Peter nodded. "That's what your brother Ferdie said."

"Ferdie knows."

"Brisley —?"

The little man waited for the question. Not wanting to hurry the boy, he got out a board and cut himself a quid of Apple Tobacco while he waited.

"It's not account of the telegraph that I got to quit now."

"No?"

"Y'see, well . . . uh . . . I just can't go back to being a pony boy. At every relay station I'd be looking for Domingo."

The question in Brislawn's eyes dissolved into insight and

compassion. "I know, I know how 'twould be. Nobody can ever go back, Peter. The past ain't ever where it used to be. *Forward* is the ticket. Today and tomorrow is what counts."

Peter let out his breath in a long sigh. "I'm thankful to you, Brisley, for making things seem right."

"No thanks atall, Peter. It's me and the whole Union that are beholden to you and all the other pony boys. You young fellers hurried the building of the telegraph by showing that if you could cross plains, deserts, and mountains, so could a little bitty string o' wire. Why, you shortened the distance 'tween the oceans till soon they'll be only a dot and a dash apart.

"What's more," he added, putting his plate down on the floor for Handy Andy, "California people, cliff-hangin' way out there over the raggedy edge of the continent, don't feel like outsiders anymore. Now they're standing with us—for the Union, strong and steady."

Peter said, "I'm thinking—that is, I *was* thinking, about being a scout in the war. Only they expect you to bring your own mount."

"No stumbling block there. I got a young horse with a yellow eye . . ." A coyote gave a long, sad howl, shutting off the talk. All three dogs pattered to the door as if their names had been called out.

"Time to bed down," Brislawn said. "I'm taking my tarp outside with the dogs. We likes the coyotes to lullabye us to sleep."

• • •

It was sweet comfort living with Brislawn, fitting into his life as if he had never been out of it. There were days of harvesting hay, enough to feed a million snowbound horses, it seemed, instead of just the half dozen in the corral.

224

One early morning Brislawn announced with a light in his eye, "I got some new critters to school. Come along and see."

Alive with curiosity, Peter helped load a wagon with fragrant hay. Blacken and Penny leaped to their lookouts atop the load. Handy Andy scrambled up on the box, wedging himself between Brislawn and Peter. And off they drove through the grass, behind two round-barreled bays.

From the matted, wheel-tracked look of the parallel lines ahead, Peter guessed the way had been traveled often. Between the tracks the grass grew high, so the trotting feet made pleasant whishing sounds. The morning mist had lifted; the hame bells on the horses' collars chimed a mellow tune, and Brislawn, looking mysteriously happy, was singing in full tenor:

> *"Oh, the Kings of Ireland*
> *They gave me birth,*
> *And I be royal too,*
> *Oh, I be royal too."*

The horses began climbing a rise now and occasionally descending a little, so that Peter was surprised when they reached the crown of a hill overlooking the prairie and came to a sudden stop. Brislawn jumped down, spry as a cricket. Making a megaphone of his hands, he yodeled for all the world to hear:

> *"Hi-leddy, hi lee,*
> *Hi-leddy, hi lo,*
> *Holeeay-ee-hee,*
> *Holeeay-ee-hoo."*

From the undulating valleys, from every direction, from as far as the eye could reach, horses came galloping toward them, tails and manes wisping along on the wind.

Brislawn meanwhile was busily forking hay everywhere, a pile here, a pile there, and nodding for Peter to do the same. The hoofbeats came closer and closer, shaking the very earth; and closer still until the knoll was suddenly alive with wildness: mares neighing, colts squealing, foals nickering, stallions nipping their mares, keeping them in a bunch. It was like a picnic with each family hungry, wanting its own place to eat in peace. But a few of the younger stallions went sneaking from hay pile to hay pile, looking for a fight and a mare to steal, and Brislawn taking off his neckerchief, using it as a direction flag to restore order. All the while he was laughing and calling this one by name and that one. "Molly dear, you've a new foal—a beaut! Hey there, Chinook, keep to your own girls." And a wave of the flag sent Chinook back where he belonged.

Peter stood spellbound. Never before had he been surrounded by horses half wild. He was right in amongst them, so close he could feel their warm breath. "Why, they're not afraid of me!" he thought. "Brisley and me—we must smell alike, of sweet dried grass. They trust us!"

The munching and grinding went on, Peter thinking it the most beautiful sound a morning could bring. Any one of the horses, he knew, could be roped and tied to the tailgate and brought home. As they flowed past and around him, he saw there was not a Medicine Hat among them. He wondered, unsure if he was sorry or relieved.

By noontime, even the wisps of hay left on the wagon bed were lipped clean.

On the way back Brislawn was strangely quiet. He seemed to be chewing on a big cud of thought.

When Peter could bear it no longer, he said, "I don't understand about the schooling. You didn't halter or lead 'em, or teach 'em anything, except how good grass is."

The little man chortled. "That's the point!" He shifted his tobacco from one cheek to the other. "Y'see, I'm schooling 'em to get used to stable eating, and how gentle man's hands and voice is. Then when Colonel Northrup comes to get them for the cavalry, they'll be half gentled for training already."

"Oh?"

"You know how quick the military is."

Peter didn't know, but listened carefully.

"Why, they break a horse quick. And then they wonder why he rolls his eyes and plasters his ears back and bucks and bites and acts ornery as a mule."

"Can I help, Brisley?"

" 'Course you can. But between our trips to the top o' the world, I'd be mighty obliged if you'd work with that young Tiger Eye in the corral. He's green as a gourd, but that rascal's got what I calls po-ten-tial!"

"You mean the dun-colored stallion with the yellow eye?"

"That's the one."

• • •

It was almost like old times, the slow day-by-day training. The sack of sand, light at first, on Tiger Eye's back. Then bit and bridle replacing halter. And finally Peter straddling the young whirlwind until he quieted down to a breeze.

Brislawn, watching from the fence rail, beamed at Peter. "Nothing to pleasure a man more," he said, "than to see a green horse come into bloom by your own hand. Eh, son?"

Peter blushed at the compliment. "Brisley . . ." he began. He kept walking the horse in a circle. Finally he stopped in front of the little man. "Brisley," he tried again, "sometimes

I feel . . ." The words came tight, wrenched from hurt. "I feel a guilt when I work with Tiger Eye."

"A *guilt?* What in the world for?"

"Seems like I'm a traitor to Domingo."

There was quietness for a time. Blacken and Penny loped into the corral and out, Andy following like a caboose.

Into the silence Brislawn said, "Yer feelings be natural as rain, right now. But horse people, as they grow older," he went on, "get to be more 'n more like parents of big families. Y'see, one amongst the younguns is bound to be the favorite. But does that stop the ma's and pa's from loving the others? No, siree! They build up love enough for all. Ain't yer feelings something like that?"

Peter was saved an answer by a horseman who turned out to be Jim Baxter, waving a letter.

"Dogberry thought you'd still be here," Jim said. He tossed the letter to Peter and was off again before any thank-you could be said.

While Brislawn looked on, Peter studied the handwriting. It was familiar, but only vaguely. He unfolded the letter and a river of fright rushed through his body when he saw it was signed "Jethro Lundy."

Ma must be sick or dying to make Pa write.

He read, and right at the start his fear turned to anger. He thrust the paper into Brislawn's hand. He too read the signature first and frowned, thinking a letter from Jethro Lundy could mean only trouble and sorrow. To postpone knowing, he took his spectacles out of his vest pocket. Carefully he fogged each lens with his breath. Deliberately he polished both to a fine shine. He adjusted the earpieces, just so. At last, rocking on his heels, he began to read. Then he stopped stock still. "Why, just listen, feller!" In the deep tones of Jethro Lundy he read aloud:

> *Peter,*
> *Belatedly, I have your letter concerning your meeting up with Slade. What I say is, you come damned near being a man.*

Brislawn handed the letter back to Peter. "Why, that's great praise! The finest! 'Tis a sight more emphatic than 'You are a man.' "

"Is it?" Peter asked, half doubtful, half wanting to believe.

"'Tis indeed! Once an old mountain man said to my son Emmett, 'You come damn near being a mountain man.' Emmett was prouder of this than if he'd been elected to be president!

"The rest of the letter," Brislawn added, "you'd best read to yourself. I might snivel, and at my age 'tain't becoming."

With hands trembling Peter took the letter and began again:

> *Belatedly, I have your letter concerning your meeting up with Slade. What I say is, you come damned near being a man. All these years I wanted you to grow up strong enough to shake off the Slades of the world. I reckon you have done it, son.*
>
> > *Your Pa,*
> > *Jethro Lundy*

Two days later, Peter rode out of Brislawn's corral on Tiger Eye. He would stop at home and meet his pa, as if for the first time. Then he would go on and enlist as a scout for the United States Army.

But scarcely out of the gate, he wanted to turn back and say all over again what he had said last night:

"I want to go home, Brisley."

"A prime idea, Peter."

"But I can't leave you here all alone. Supposin' you was to sicken and . . ."

"And no one to bury me and carve my name? Pshaw," Brislawn had laughed, "my name's printed big in little weeping clouds and thumping thunder and grand lightning. And down in my root cellar"—here his eye twinkled in enjoyment—"they'll find rib cages of my Spanish Barb horses, proving to the whole dang world that the pure Barb ponies have just five lumbar vertebrae like their Spanish forebears. What better nameplate than provin' something in your lifetime?

"You best go on, Peter," he urged. "You are all I have of the future. And don't you go feeling sorry for me. Autumn's a good time of life, too. Quakenasp and goldenrod turning yellow, and purple sage smelling nice. So fall is here, and my old bed tarp is here. And someday I'll take the long trail with my critters to their blue bunchgrass heaven . . . and in time you'll come along, too."

After long moments of reliving all that had been said, Peter *had* to turn around to look. Even with the remembrance of words from another time of parting: " 'Tis an old Irish taboo, Peter. Don't watch me out of sight, or we'll never set eyes on each other again—in this world."

The compulsion was too strong. Peter turned. He had to. And he saw the little man, his big hat lifted high in Peter's direction. They were each watching the other out of sight.

For their help the author is grateful to

DR. GENE M. GRESSLEY, Director, The University
   of Wyoming Western History Research Center

JEFF EDWARDS, authority on the Spanish Barb horse,
   Porterville, California

DAVID MILLER, authority on the Sioux language,
   Rancho Santa Fe, California

ABEDNEGO MEARS, collector of old firearms

HENRY E. HUNTINGTON LIBRARY, San Marino, California

RANCHO SANTA FE PUBLIC LIBRARY,
   Rancho Santa Fe, California

SAN DIEGO COUNTY LIBRARY, San Diego, California

ST. CHARLES PUBLIC LIBRARY, St. Charles, Illinois

Books Consulted

Anderson, William Marshall, *The Rocky Mountain Journals of William Marshall Anderson*

Back, Joe, *Horses, Hitches and Rocky Trails*

Booker, William Saul, letter dated April 23, 1860, in *The Illustrated London News*, October 12, 1861; articles by British Consul in San Francisco in 1860

Bowman, John Gabbert, *The World That Was*

Burton, Sir Richard F., *The City of the Saints*

Carpenter, Helen M., hand-written diary, *Trip across the plains, 1857*

Colum, Padraic, editor, *Treasury of Irish Folklore*

Crane, A. M., *Journal of a trip across the plains, 1852*

Dick, Everett, *The Sod-House Frontier, 1854–1890*

Eckert, Allan W., *The Frontiersman*

Ellison, Robert S., *Fort Bridger, Wyoming, A Brief History*

Ellison, Robert S., *Independence Rock—The Great Record of the Desert*

Erwin, M. H., *Wyoming Historical Blue Book*

Federal Writers Project, *Oregon Trail: The Missouri River to the Pacific Ocean*

Federal Writers Project, *Wyoming; Guide to Its History, Highways and People*

Gorsline, Douglas Warner, *What People Wore; a visual history of dress from ancient times to twentieth century America*

Hendricks, Carl Brehains, *Compilation of Outlaws*

Josephy, Alvin M., Jr., editor, *The Great West*

Larson, T. A., *History of Wyoming*

Lavender, David, *Westward Vision: The Story of the Oregon Trail*

McClinton, Katharine Morrison, *Antiques of American Childhood*

Majors, Alexander, *Seventy Years on the Frontier*

Parke, Charles R., *Journal of a trip across the plains*

Parkman, Francis, *The Oregon Trail*

Peterson, Harold L., *Forts in America*

Point, Father Nicholas, S.J., *Wilderness Kingdom, The Journals of Father Nicholas Point, S.J., Indian Life in the Rocky Mountains*, trans. by Joseph P. Donnelly

Rollinson, John K., *Hoofprints of a cowboy and U.S. ranger; pony trails in Wyoming*

Root, Frank A., and Connelley, William Elsey, *The Overland Stage to California*

Sandburg, Carl, *Abraham Lincoln, The War Years*

Spring, Agnes Wright, *The Cheyenne and Black Hills Stage and Express Routes*

Stegner, Wallace E., *The Gathering of Zion, The Story of the Mormon Trail*

Vodges, Ada A., *Journal describing life of an army officer's wife at Ft. Laramie and Ft. Fetterman*

Walker, Henry Pickering, *The Wagonmasters: High Plains Freighting from the Earliest Days of the Santa Fe Trail to 1880*

Warp, Harold, *A History of Man's Progress from 1830 to the Present*

Watson, A. A., *The Village Blacksmith*

Welsh, John P., diary, *Overland journey from Wisconsin to Oregon, 1851–1863*

Wenstrom, William Holmes, *Weather and the Ocean of Air*

Wilkins, James F., *An Artist on the Overland Trail*

Wood, Joseph N., hand-written diary